Books by Joan Didion

A Book of Common Prayer
Play It As It Lays
Run River

Published by POCKET BOOKS

JOAN DIDION
PLAY IT AS IT LAYS

PUBLISHED BY POCKET BOOKS NEW YORK

POCKET BOOKS, a Simon & Schuster division of
GULF & WESTERN CORPORATION
1230 Avenue of the Americas, New York, N.Y. 10020

ISBN: 0-671-82219-5

First Pocket Books printing October, 1978

Trademarks registered in the United States and other countries.

Printed in the U.S.A.

FOR JOHN

PLAY IT AS IT LAYS

MARIA

WHAT MAKES IAGO EVIL? some people ask. I never
ask.

Another example, one which springs to mind because Mrs. Burstein saw a pygmy rattler in the arti-
choke garden this morning and has been intractable
since: I never ask about snakes. Why should Shalimar
attract kraits. Why should a coral snake need two
glands of neurotoxic poison to survive while a king
snake, *so similarly marked,* needs none. Where is the
Darwinian logic there. You might ask that. I never
would, not any more. I recall an incident reported not
long ago in the Los Angeles *Herald-Examiner:* two
honeymooners, natives of Detroit, found dead in their
Scout camper near Boca Raton, a coral snake still
coiled in the thermal blanket. Why? Unless you are
prepared to take the long view, there is no satisfac-
tory "answer" to such questions.

Just so. I am what I am. To look for "reasons" is
beside the point. But because the pursuit of reasons

is their business here, they ask me questions. Maria, yes or no: I see a cock in this inkblot. Maria, yes or no: A large number of people are guilty of bad sexual conduct, I believe my sins are unpardonable, I have been disappointed in love. How could I answer? How could it apply? NOTHING APPLIES, I print with the magnetized IBM pencil. What does apply, they ask later, as if the word "nothing" were ambiguous, open to interpretation, a questionable fragment of an Icelandic rune. There are only certain facts, I say, trying again to be an agreeable player of the game. Certain facts, certain things that happened. (Why bother, you might ask. I bother for Kate. What I play for here is Kate. Carter put Kate in there and I am going to get her out.) They will misread the facts, invent connections, will extrapolate reasons where none exist, but I told you, that is their business here.

So they suggested that I set down the facts, and the facts are these: My name is Maria Wyeth. That is pronounced Mar-*eye*-ah, to get it straight at the outset. Some people here call me "Mrs. Lang," but I never did. Age, thirty-one. Married. Divorced. One daughter, age four. (I talk about Kate to no one here. In the place where Kate is they put electrodes on her head and needles in her spine and try to figure what went wrong. It is one more version of why does a coral snake have two glands of neurotoxic poison. Kate has soft down on her spine and an aberrant chemical in her brain. Kate is Kate. Carter could not remember the soft down on her spine or he would not let them put needles there.) From my mother I inherited my looks and a tendency to migraine. From my father I inherited an optimism which did not leave me until recently.

Details: I was born in Reno, Nev., and moved nine years later to Silver Wells, Nev., pop. then 28, now 0. We moved down to Silver Wells because my father lost the Reno house in a private game and happened to remember that he owned this town, Silver Wells. He had bought it or won it or maybe his father left it to him, I'm not sure which and it doesn't matter to you. We had a lot of things and places that came and went, a cattle ranch with no cattle and a ski resort picked up on somebody's second mortgage and a motel that would have been advantageously situated at a freeway exit had the freeway been built; I was raised to believe that what came in on the next roll would always be better than what went out on the last. I no longer believe that, but I am telling you how it was. What we had in Silver Wells was three hundred acres of mesquite and some houses and a Flying A and a zinc mine and a Tonopah & Tidewater RR siding and a trinket shop and later, after my father and his partner Benny Austin hit on the idea that Silver Wells was a natural tourist attraction, a midget golf course and a reptile museum and a restaurant with some slots and two crap tables. The slots were not exactly moneymakers because the only person who played them was Paulette, with nickels from the cash-box. Paulette ran the restaurant and (I see now) balled my father and sometimes let me pretend to cashier after school. I say "pretend" because there were no customers. As it happened the highway my father counted on came nowhere near and the money ran out and my mother got sick and Benny Austin went back to Vegas, I ran into him in the Flamingo a few years ago. "Your father's only Waterloo was he was a man always twenty years before his time," Benny advised me that night in the Flamingo. "The ghost-town scheme, the midget golf, the automatic black-jack concept, what do you see today? Harry Wyeth could be a *Rock*efeller in Silver Wells today."

"There isn't any Silver Wells today," I said. "It's in the middle of a missile range."

"I'm speaking about *then*, Maria. *As it was.*"

Benny called for a round of Cuba Libres, a drink I have never known anyone but my mother and father and Benny Austin to order, and I gave him some chips to play for me and went to the ladies' room and never came back. I told myself it was because I didn't want Benny to see the kind of man I was with, I was with a man who was playing baccarat with hundred-dollar bills behind the rope, but that wasn't all of it. I might as well lay it on the line, I have trouble with *as it was.*

I mean it leads nowhere. Benny Austin, my mother sitting in Paulette's empty restaurant when it was 120° outside looking through her magazines for contests we could enter (Waikiki, Paris France, Roman Holiday, my mother's yearnings suffused our life like nerve gas, *cross the ocean in a silver plane,* she would croon to herself and mean it, *see the jungle when it's wet with rain*), the three of us driving down to Vegas in the pickup and then driving home again in the clear night, a hundred miles down and a hundred back and nobody on the highway either way, just the snakes stretched on the warm asphalt and my mother with a wilted gardenia in her dark hair and my father keeping a fifth of Jim Beam on the floorboard and talking about his plans, he always had a lot of plans, I never in my life had any plans, none of it makes any sense, none of it adds up.

New York: what sense did that make? An eighteen-year-old girl from Silver Wells, Nevada, graduates from the Consolidated Union High School in Tonopah and goes to New York to take acting lessons, how do you figure it? My mother thought being an actress was a nice idea, she used to cut my hair in bangs to look like Margaret Sullavan, and my father said not to be afraid to go because if certain deals worked out as anticipated he and my mother would be regular airline passengers between Las Vegas and New York City, so I went. As it turned out, the last time but once I ever saw my mother was sitting in the Vegas airport drinking a Cuba Libre, but there you are. Everything goes. I am working very hard at not thinking about how everything goes. I watch a hummingbird, throw the I Ching but never read the coins, keep my mind in the now. New York. Let me stick to certain facts. What happened was this: I looked all right (I'm not telling you I was blessed or cursed, I'm telling a fact, I know it from all the pictures) and somebody photographed me and before long I was getting $100 an hour from the agencies and $50 from the magazines which in those days was not bad and I knew a lot of Southerners and faggots and rich boys and that was how I spent my days and nights. The night my mother ran the car off the highway outside Tonopah I was with a drunk rich boy at the old Morocco, as close as I could figure later: I didn't know about it for a couple of weeks because the coyotes tore her up before anybody found her and my father couldn't tell me. ("Jesus but we had a good thing going in Silver Wells,"

Benny Austin said that night in the Flamingo, and maybe they did, maybe I did, maybe I never should have left, but that line of thinking leads nowhere because as I told Benny *there is no Silver Wells*. The last I heard of Paulette she was living in a Sun City. Think that one over.) My father's letter was mailed to an old address and forwarded, I read it in a taxi one morning when I was late for a sitting and when I hit the fact in the middle of the second paragraph I began to scream and did not work for a month after. The letter is still in my makeup box but I am careful not to read it unless I am drunk, which in my current situation is never. "This is a bad hand but God if there is one, and Honey I sincerely believe there must be 'Something', never meant it to set you back in your Plans," is how it ends. "Don't let them bluff you back there because you're holding all the aces."

Easy aces. I am not sure what year it was because I have this problem with *as it was,* but after a while I had a bad time. (There, you will say now, she believed her sins were unpardonable, but I told you, nothing applies.) The tulips on Park Avenue looked dirty and I was sent twice to Montego Bay to get some color back in my face but I could not sleep alone and stayed up late and it was falling apart with

Ivan Costello and everything showed in the camera by then. Of course I did not get back to Nevada that year because that was the year I screamed at Ivan and married Carter, and the next was the year we came here and Carter put me in a couple of little pictures (one you may have seen, a doctor here claims to have seen it but he will say anything to make me talk, the other never distributed) and I don't know what happened the year after that and then I started getting to Nevada quite a bit, but by then my father was dead and I was not married any more.

Those are the facts. Now I lie in the sun and play solitaire and listen to the sea (the sea is down the cliff but I am not allowed to swim, only on Sundays when we are accompanied) and watch a humming-bird. I try not to think of dead things and plumbing. I try not to hear the air conditioner in that bedroom in Encino. I try not to live in Silver Wells or in New York or with Carter. I try to live in the now and keep my eye on the hummingbird. I see no one I used to know, but then I'm not just crazy about a lot of people. I mean maybe I was holding all the aces, but what was the game?

HELENE

I SAW MARIA TODAY. Or at least I tried to see Maria today: I made the effort. I didn't make it for Maria I don't mind saying, I made it for Carter, or for BZ, or for old times or for something, not for Maria. "I don't much want to talk to you, Helene," was what she said the last time. "It's not personal, Helene, I just don't talk any more." Not for Maria.

Anyway I didn't. See her. I drove all the way out there, took the entire morning and packed a box for her, all the new books and a chiffon scarf she left at the beach once (she was careless, it must have cost thirty dollars, she was always careless) and a pound of caviar, maybe not Beluga but Maria shouldn't bitch now, plus a letter from Ivan Costello and a long profile somebody did in *The New York Times* about Carter, you'd think that would at least interest her except Maria has never been able to bear Carter's success, all that, and Maria wouldn't see me. "Mrs. Lang is resting," the nurse said. I could see her resting, I could see her down by the pool in the same bikini she was wearing the summer she killed BZ, lying by that swimming pool with a shade over her eyes as if she hadn't a care or a responsibility in the world. She never puts on any weight, you'll notice that's often true of selfish women. Not that I blame Maria for anything that happened to me, although I'm the one who suffered, I'm the one who should be "resting," I'm the one who lost BZ through her carelessness, her selfishness, but I blame her only *on Carter's behalf*. Half a chance and she would have killed Carter too. She was always a very selfish girl, it was first last and always Maria.

CARTER

HERE ARE SOME SCENES I have very clear in my mind.

"I always get breakfast out," I say to someone. This is at a dinner party, a group of friends. Maria would say that they were not her friends, but Maria has never understood friendship, conversation, the normal amenities of social exchange. Maria has difficulty talking to people with whom she is not sleeping.

"I go to the Wilshire or the Beverly Hills," I say. "I read the trades, I like to be alone at breakfast."

"In fact he doesn't always get breakfast out," Maria says, very low, to no one in particular. "In fact the last time he got breakfast out was on April 17."

The others at the table look first at her and then away, astonished, uneasy: something in the way her hands are tensed on the edge of the table prevents passing this off. Only BZ continues to look directly at her.

"Oh fuck it," she says then, and tears run down her

cheeks. She still looks very straight ahead at no one in particular.

Another scene: she is playing on the lawn with the baby, tossing up drops of water from a clear plastic hose. "Watch out she doesn't get chilled," I say from the terrace; Maria looks up, drops the hose, and walks away from the baby toward the poolhouse. She turns, and looks back at the baby. "Your father wants to talk to you," she says. Her voice is neutral.

After BZ's death there was a time when I played and replayed these scenes and others like them, composed them as if for the camera, trying to find some order, a pattern. I found none. All I can say is this: it was after a succession of such small scenes that I began to see the improbability of a rapprochement with Maria.

1

In the first hot month of the fall after the summer she left Carter (the summer Carter left her, the summer Carter stopped living in the house in Beverly Hills), Maria drove the freeway. She dressed every morning with a greater sense of purpose than she had felt in some time, a cotton skirt, a jersey, sandals she could kick off when she wanted the touch of the accelerator, and she dressed very fast, running a brush through her hair once or twice and tying it back with a ribbon, for it was essential (to pause was to throw herself into unspeakable peril) that she be on the freeway by ten o'clock. Not somewhere on Hollywood Boulevard, not on her way to the freeway, but actually on the freeway. If she was not she lost the day's rhythm, its precariously imposed momentum. Once she was on the freeway and had maneuvered her way to a fast lane she turned on the radio at high volume and she drove. She drove the San Diego to the

Harbor, the Harbor up to the Hollywood, the Hollywood to the Golden State, the Santa Monica, the
Santa Ana, the Pasadena, the Ventura. She drove it
as a riverman runs a river, every day more attuned
to its currents, its deceptions, and just as a riverman
feels the pull of the rapids in the lull between sleeping and waking, so Maria lay at night in the still of
Beverly Hills and saw the great signs soar overhead
at seventy miles an hour, *Normandie ¼ Vermont ¾
Harbor Fwy* 1. Again and again she returned to an
intricate stretch just south of the interchange where
successful passage from the Hollywood onto the Harbor required a diagonal move across four lanes of
traffic. On the afternoon she finally did it without once
braking or once losing the beat on the radio she was
exhilarated, and that night slept dreamlessly. By then
she was sleeping not in the house but out by the pool,
on a faded rattan chaise left by a former tenant. There
was a jack for a telephone there, and she used beach
towels for blankets. The beach towels had a special
point. Because she had an uneasy sense that sleeping
outside on a rattan chaise could be construed as the
first step toward something unnameable (she did not
know what it was she feared, but it had to do with
empty sardine cans in the sink, vermouth bottles in
the wastebaskets, slovenliness past the point of re-

turn) she told herself that she was sleeping outside just until it was too cold to sleep beneath beach towels, just until the heat broke, just until the fires stopped burning in the mountains, sleeping outside only because the bedrooms in the house were hot, airless, only because the palms scraped against the screens and there was no one to wake her in the mornings. The beach towels signified how temporary the arrangement was. Outside she did not have to be afraid that she would not wake up, outside she could sleep. Sleep was essential if she was to be on the freeway by ten o'clock. Sometimes the freeway ran out, in a scrap metal yard in San Pedro or on the main street of Palmdale or out somewhere no place at all where the flawless burning concrete just stopped, turned into common road, abandoned construction sheds rusting beside it. When that happened she would keep in careful control, portage skillfully back, feel for the first time the heavy weight of the becalmed car beneath her and try to keep her eyes on the mainstream, the great pilings, the Cyclone fencing, the deadly oleander, the luminous signs, the organism which absorbed all her reflexes, all her attention.

So that she would not have to stop for food she kept a hard-boiled egg on the passenger seat of the Corvette. She could shell and eat a hard-boiled egg at seventy miles an hour (crack it on the steering wheel, never mind salt, salt bloats, no matter what happened she remembered her body) and she drank Coca-Cola in Union 76 stations, Standard stations, Flying A's. She would stand on the hot pavement and drink the Coke from the bottle and put the bottle back in the rack (she tried always to let the attendant notice her putting the bottle in the rack, a show of thoughtful responsibility, no sardine cans in her sink) and then she would walk to the edge of the concrete and stand, letting the sun dry her damp back. To hear her own voice she would sometimes talk to the attendant, ask advice on oil filters, how much air the tires should carry, the most efficient route to Foothill Boulevard in West Covina. Then she would retie the ribbon in her hair and rinse her dark glasses in the drinking fountain and be ready to drive again. In the first hot month of the fall after the summer she left Carter, the summer Carter left her, the summer Carter stopped living in the house in Beverly Hills, a bad season in the city, Maria put seven thousand miles on the Corvette. Sometimes at night the dread would overtake her, bathe her in sweat, flood her mind with sharp flash images of Les Goodwin in New York and Carter out there on the desert with BZ and Helene and the irrevocability of what seemed already to have happened, but she never thought about that on the freeway.

2

THE SECOND PICTURE she had made with Carter was called *Angel Beach*, and in it she played a girl who was raped by the members of a motorcycle gang. Carter had brought the picture in for $340,000 and the studio had saturation-booked it and by the end of the first year the domestic and foreign gross was just under eight million dollars. Maria had seen it twice, once at a studio preview and a second time by herself, at a drive-in in Culver City, and neither time did she have any sense that the girl on the screen was herself. "I look at you and I know that . . . *what happened* just didn't mean anything," the girl on the screen would say, and "There's a lot more to living than just kicks, I see that now, kicks are nowhere." Carter's original cut ended with a shot of the motorcycle gang, as if they represented some reality not fully apprehended by the girl Maria played, but the cut released by the studio ended with a long dolly shot of Maria strolling across a campus. Maria preferred the studio's cut. In fact, she liked watching the picture: the girl on the screen seemed to have a definite knack for controlling her own destiny.

The other picture, the first picture, the picture never distributed, was called *Maria*. Carter had simply followed Maria around New York and shot film. It was not until they moved to California and Carter began cutting the film together that she entirely realized what he was doing. The picture showed Maria doing a fashion sitting, Maria asleep on a couch at a party, Maria on the telephone arguing with the billing department at Bloomingdale's, Maria cleaning some marijuana with a kitchen strainer, Maria crying on the IRT. At the end she was thrown into negative and looked dead. The picture lasted seventy-four minutes and had won a prize at a festival in Eastern Europe and Maria did not like to look at it. She had once heard that students at UCLA and USC talked about using her the way commercial directors talked about using actresses who got a million dollars a picture, but she had never talked to any of them (sometimes they walked up to Carter in front of a theater or a bookstore and introduced themselves, and Carter would introduce Maria, and they would look sidelong at Maria while they talked to Carter about coming to see their film programs, but Maria had nothing to say to them, avoided their eyes) and she disliked their having seen her in that first picture. She never thought of it as *Maria*. She thought of it always as that first picture. Carter took her to BZ and Helene's one night when BZ was running the picture and she had to leave the house after the titles, had to sit outside on the beach smoking cigarettes and fighting nausea for seventy-two of the seventy-four minutes.

"Why does he run it so often," she had said to Carter later. "Why do you let him keep a print out there, he *keeps a print in the house.*"

"He owns it, Maria. He owns all the prints."

"That's not what I mean. I said why does he run it so often."

"He wants Helene to see it."

"Helene's seen it a dozen times. Helene doesn't even *like* it, she told me so."

"You don't understand anything," Carter had said finally, and they had gone to bed that night without speaking. Maria did not want to understand why BZ ran that first picture so often or what it had to do with Helene. The girl on the screen in that first picture had no knack for anything.

3

"MARIA WYETH," she repeated to Freddy Chaikin's receptionist. The reception room was full of glossy plants in chinoiserie pots and Maria had an abrupt conviction that the plants were consuming the oxygen she needed to breathe. She should not have come here without calling. Only people in trouble came unannounced to see their agents. If Freddy Chaikin thought she carried trouble with her he would avoid her, because trouble was something no one in the city liked to be near. Failure, illness, fear, they were seen as infectious, contagious blights on glossy plants. It seemed to Maria that even the receptionist was avoiding her eyes, fearing contamination. "He's kind of expecting me," Maria added in a near whisper.

"Maria Wyeth," the receptionist said. "Mr. Chaikin is in the projection room, do you want to wait? Or could he call you."

"No. I mean yes. But tell him it has to be today or—"

The receptionist waited.

"Or I'll talk to him tomorrow," Maria said finally.

In the elevator was an actor she recognized but had never met, the star of a canceled television Western. He was with a short agent in a narrow dark suit, and the agent smiled at Maria as the elevator door closed.

"The word on Carter's dailies is sensational," the agent said.

Maria smiled and nodded. It did not require an answer: it was a cue for the actor, who waited a suitable instant and then picked it up. "Your pocketbook's open," he drawled, and the look he gave Maria was dutifully charged with sexual appreciation, meant not for Maria herself but for Carter Lang's wife. She leaned against the padded elevator wall and closed her eyes. If she could tell Les Goodwin about the actor in the elevator he would laugh. When she got home she thought about calling him, but instead she went upstairs and lay face down on Kate's empty bed, cradled Kate's blanket, clutched Kate's baby pillow to her stomach and fought off a wave of the dread. The time seemed to have passed for telling Les Goodwin funny stories.

4

She sat on the rattan chaise in the hot October twilight and watched BZ throw the ice cubes from his drink one by one into the swimming pool. They had already talked about Helene's week at La Costa and they had already talked about an actress who had been admitted to UCLA Neuropsychiatric with her wrists cut (the papers said exhaustion, but BZ knew things like that, knew about people, that was why she had called him) and now it was the hour when in all the houses all around the pretty women were putting on perfume and enameled bracelets and kissing the pretty children goodnight, the hour of apparent grace and promised music, and even here in Maria's own garden the air smelled of jasmine and the water in the pool was 85°. The water in the pool was always 85° and it was always clean. It came with the rent. Whether or not Carter could afford the rent, whether it was a month like this one when he was making a lot of money or a month when the lawyers were talking about bankruptcy, the boy came twice a week to vacuum the pool and the man came four days a week to work on the roses and the water in the pool was 85°. Sometimes it occurred to Maria that maybe the pretty children and the enameled bracelets came the same way, but she did not like to think about that.

"Tell me who you've seen," she said. She did not much want to hear who BZ had seen but neither did she want BZ to leave. BZ had not yet mentioned Carter. BZ was the producer on the picture, BZ had come in from the location two days before and he was going back to the location tomorrow and he had not once mentioned Carter. "Tell me about the Willards' dance."

"Strobe lights in Pasadena." BZ stood up. "On nights like that you could kill yourself for being a Gentile."

"Don't leave."

"I'm late now. I'm supposed to be somewhere."

"Who is it," she said, not looking at him.

"Nobody special, I'm meeting Tommy Loew, you know Tommy, he's in from New York."

"I don't mean you." She wondered without interest if Tommy Loew was a faggot. "You know I don't mean you."

"I don't know what you're talking about." BZ put

24

his glass on a table, and looked at Maria for a long while. "Just let him finish."

"Who is it." She did not know why she persisted.

"Listen, Maria. I don't know if you know this, but he wanted you in this picture very badly. At one point he was ready to scrap the deal, jeopardize the entire project, just because he wanted to use you."

"I know that."

"Then why not stop thinking Carter designs his every move expressly to thwart you. Why not stop thinking like Carlotta."

"You don't have any idea in your mind how I think." Carlotta was BZ's mother. Carlotta had $35 million and was engaged in constant litigation with her estranged second husband. Maria sat down on the edge of the pool and splashed the clear water over her bare feet. "Listen to the music from the Kuliks'. They're having a party."

"You going?"

"Of course I'm not going. He's a gangster."

"I just asked if you were going to a party, Maria, I didn't ask for a grand-jury indictment." BZ paused. "In the second place he's not a gangster. He's a lawyer."

"For gangsters."

BZ shrugged. "I think of him more as a philosopher king. He told me once he understood the whole meaning of life, it came to him in a blinding flash one time when he almost died on the table at Cedars."

"Larry Kulik's not going to die at Cedars. Larry Kulik's going to die in a barber chair."

"It's uphill work making you laugh, Maria. Anyway, Larry Kulik's a great admirer of yours. You know what he said to Carter? He said, 'What I like about your wife, Carter, is she's not a cunt.' "

Maria said nothing.

"That's very funny, Maria, Kulik saying that to Carter, you lost your sense of humor?"

"I've already heard it. Give me your glass."

"I told you, Tommy Loew. I'm already late."

"Who is it," she repeated.

"He's two weeks behind schedule now, Maria. Just let him finish the picture." BZ stood up, and ran the tips of his fingers very lightly across Maria's bare back. "Seen anything of Les Goodwin?" he said finally.

Maria watched a leaf in the water and tried not to recoil from BZ's fingers. "Les and Felicia are in New York," she said carefully, and then reached for a towel. "You're already late for Tommy Loew, I mean aren't you?"

Later in the week she saw in one of the columns that BZ had been at the Kuliks' party with Tommy Loew and a starlet whose name she did not recognize.

She did not know why it annoyed her but it did. She wondered if Tommy Loew and the starlet had gone back to BZ's later, and who had watched whom, and if Helene had been back from La Costa.

5

"Just wanted you to know I'm thinking of you," Freddy Chaikin said on the telephone. "I'll be frank, I was surprised to hear you wanted to work again. After that debacle with Mark Ross, I just naturally thought—"

"I've always wanted to work." Maria tried to keep her voice even. Freddy would be sitting in his office with the Barcelona chairs and the Giacometti sculpture and anything he wanted to say Maria would have to hear.

"—an actress walks off a set, people tend to think she doesn't want to work."

"That was almost a year ago. I was sick. I was upset about Kate. I haven't walked off any more sets, you *know* that, Freddy."

"You haven't had any sets *to* walk off."

Maria closed her eyes. "What are you doing right now, Freddy," she said finally. "You sitting there playing with a Fabergé Easter egg? Or what?"

"Calm down. Actually I talked to Morty Landau about you today at lunch. I said, Morty, you know Maria Wyeth, and he did—"

"I should think so. I had the lead in two features."

"Right, Maria, of course you did. You know that. I know that. And they were very interesting little pictures. Carter parlayed those two little pictures, one of them never distributed, into a very nice thing. Carter's in the enviable position now where he wants to do something, it's just a question of working out the numbers. I'm proud to represent him. I'm proud to represent both of you, Maria. Maybe I could arrange for Morty Landau to see some film, you give me your word that you really want to work."

"See some *film*."

"Where's the problem, Maria? There's something so unusual about wanting to see some film? I show film on talent getting two, two-fifty a picture."

"Morty Landau makes television."

"Let's get to the bottom line, Maria, if Carter were around he'd say the same thing. You want to work, I'll arrange for Morty Landau to see film."

"Carter is around."

There was a silence, and when Freddy Chaikin spoke again his voice was gentle. "All I meant, Maria, was that Carter's on location. All I meant."

6

ON THE TENTH DAY OF OCTOBER at quarter past four in the afternoon with a dry hot wind blowing through the passes Maria found herself in Baker. She had never meant to go as far as Baker, had started out that day as every day, her only destination the freeway. But she had driven out the San Bernardino and up the Barstow and instead of turning back at Barstow (she had been out that far before but never that late in the day, it was past time to navigate back, she was out too far too late, the rhythm was lost) she kept driving. When she turned off at Baker it was 115° and she was picking up Vegas on the radio and she was within sixty miles of where Carter was making the picture. He could be in the motel right now. They could be through shooting for the day and he could be having a drink with BZ and Helene, thinking about going into Vegas for dinner or just resting, resting on the unmade bed with his shirt off. The woman who ran the motel only made the beds once a week, Carter had made a joke about it in an interview, Maria had read it in the trades. She could call. "Listen," she could say. "I'm in Baker. I just happen to be in Baker."

"So you just happen to be in Baker," he could say. "Get on up here."

Or he could even say: "Listen. Get up here quick."

Those were things he could say but because she did not know if he would say them or even if she wanted to hear them she just sat in the car behind the 76 station in Baker and studied the pay phone by the Coke machine. Whatever he began by saying he would end by saying nothing. He would say something and she would say something and before either of them knew it they would be playing out a dialogue so familiar that it drained the imagination, blocked the will, allowed them to drop words and whole sentences and still arrive at the cold conclusion. "Oh Christ," he would say. "I felt good today, really good for a change, you fixed that, you really pricked the balloon."

"How did I fix that."

"You know how."

"I don't know how."

She would wait for him to answer but he would say nothing then, would just sit with his head in his hands. She would feel first guilty, resigned to misery, then furious, trapped, white with anger. "*Listen* to me," she would say then, almost shouting, trying to take him by the shoulders and shake him out of what she could not see as other than an elaborate pose; he would knock her away, and the look on his face, contorted, teeth bared, would render her paralyzed. "Why don't you just get it over with," he would say then, leaning close, his face still contorted. "Why don't you just go in that bathroom and take every pill in it. Why don't you die."

After that he would leave for a while, breaking things as he went, slamming doors to kick them open, picking up decanters to hurl at mirrors, detouring by way of chairs to smash them against the floor. Always when he came back he would sleep in their room, shutting the door against her. Rigid with self-pity she would lie in another room, wishing for the will to leave. Each believed the other a murderer of time, a destroyer of life itself. She did not know what she was doing in Baker. However it began it ended like that.

"Listen," she would say.

"Don't touch me," he would say.

Maria looked at the pay phone for a long while, and then she got out of the car and drank a warm Coke. With the last of the Coke she swallowed two Fiorinal tablets, then closed her eyes against the sun and waited for the Fiorinal to clear her head of Carter and what Carter would say. On the way back into the city the traffic was heavy and the hot wind blew sand through the windows and the radio got on her nerves and after that Maria did not go back to the freeway except as a way of getting somewhere.

7

"C'EST MOI, MARIA," the voice said on the telephone. "BZ."

Maria tried to untangle the cord from the receiver and fight her way out of sleep. Sleeping in the afternoon was a bad sign. She had been trying not to notice the signs but she could not avoid this one, and a sharp fear contracted her stomach muscles. "Where are you," she said finally.

"At the beach."

Maria groped on the edge of the pool for her dark glasses.

"Did I catch you in the middle of an overdose, Maria? Or what?"

"I thought you were on the desert."

"We're shutting down for a week, don't you read the trades? Because of the fire."

"What fire."

"On top of the news as ever," BZ said. "The fire, we had a fire, we have to rebuild the set. Carter's coming in tomorrow. I'll take you to Anita Garson's tonight if you're not doing anything, all right?"

"Where's Helene?"

"Helene's in bed, Helene's depressed. Helene has these very *cop*ious menstruations." There was a pause. "Seven-thirty all right?"

"I don't know about Anita Garson's, I don't—"

"I meant of course unless you've got *plans.*" His voice rose almost imperceptibly. "Unless you've got an *à deux* going at the Marmont. Or wherever it is he stays."

Maria said nothing.

"You're a lot of laughs this afternoon, Maria, I'm glad I called. I just meant that you and Les Goodwin were friends. As in just-good. No innuendo. No offense." He paused. "You still sulking in there?"

"I'll see you at seven-thirty," she said finally.

Later she could not think how she had been coerced by BZ into going to Anita Garson's party, which was large and noisy and crowded with people she did not much like. There was a rock group and a pink tent and everywhere Maria looked she saw someone who registered on her only as a foreigner or a faggot or a gangster. She tried to keep her eyes bright and her lips slightly parted and she stayed close to BZ. "How's Carter," someone said behind her, and when she turned she saw that it was Larry Kulik.

"Carter's on location," she said, but Larry Kulik was not listening. He was watching a very young girl in a white halter dress dancing on the terrace.

"I'd like to get into that," he said contemplatively to BZ.

"I wouldn't call it the impossible dream," BZ said.

Maria twisted the napkin around her glass. She had already smiled too long and she did not want to look any more at Larry Kulik's careful manicure and expensively tailored suit and she did not want to consider why Larry Kulik was talking to BZ about the girl in the white dress.

"Not that many guys," Larry Kulik was saying. "Not just anybody."

"Shit no. You have to be able to get her into the Whisky."

Larry Kulik was still watching the girl. "Only six guys."

"How do you know, six?"

Larry Kulik shrugged. "I had her researched. Six." He patted Maria's arm absently. "How's it going, baby? How's Carter?"

At the table on the terrace where Maria and BZ sat for dinner there were a French director, his cinematographer, and two English Lesbians who lived in Santa Monica Canyon. Maria sat next to the cinematographer, who spoke no English, and during dinner BZ and the French director disappeared into the house. Maria could smell marijuana, but it was not mentioned on the terrace. The cinematographer and the two Lesbians discussed the dehumanizing aspect of American technology, in French.

"You have to come over sometime and use the sauna," Larry Kulik said when he brushed by the table on his way inside. "Stereo piped in, beaucoup fantastic."

At midnight one of the amplifiers broke down, and the band packed up to leave. BZ was getting together a group to go back to his house: the French director, Larry Kulik, the girl in the white halter dress. "Simplicity itself," he said to Maria. "The chickie wants the frog."

"I have to go home."

"You're not exactly a shot of meth tonight anyway."

"I feel beaucoup fantastic," Maria said, and turned her face away so that he would not see her tears. When Les Goodwin called from New York the next morning at seven o'clock she began to cry again. Why was she crying, he wanted to know. Because he made her so happy, she said, and for that moment believed it.

8

"You haven't asked me how it went after we left Anita's," BZ said.

"How did it go," Maria said without interest.

"Everybody got what he came for."

"Don't you ever get tired of doing favors for people?"

There was a long silence. "You don't know how tired," BZ said.

9

She looked at carter sitting in the living room and all she could think was that he had put on weight. The blue work shirt he was wearing pulled at the buttons. She supposed that he had weighed that much when he left, she noticed it now only because she had not seen him.

"You going to stay here?" she said.

He rubbed his knuckles across the stubble on his chin. "All my things are here, aren't they?"

Maria sat down across from him. She wished she had a cigarette but there were none on the table and it seemed frivolous to go get one. Carter's saying that all his things were in the house did not seem entirely conclusive, did not address itself to the question. Quite often with Carter she felt like Ingrid Bergman in *Gaslight,* another frivolous thought.

"I mean I thought we were kind of separated." That did not sound exactly right either.

"If that's the way you want it."

"It wasn't me. I mean was it me?"

"Never, Maria. Never you."

There was a silence. Something real was happening: this was, as it were, her life. If she could keep that in mind she would be able to play it through, do the right thing, whatever that meant.

"I guess we could try," she said uncertainly.

"Only if you want to."

"Of course I do." She did not know what else to say. "Of course I want to."

"Why don't you sound like it."

"Carter, I *do*." She paused, abruptly exhausted. "Maybe it's not such a good idea."

"Do what you want," he said, and went upstairs.

Maria sat with her eyes closed until the vein in her temple stopped pulsing, then followed him upstairs. He lay on the bed in their room, staring at the ceiling. Only by an increased immobility did he acknowledge her presence.

"I was going out to see Kate," she said finally.

"How many times you been out there lately?" He still did not look at her.

"Hardly at all," she said, and then: "In the past few weeks, maybe a couple of times."

"You've been there four times since Sunday."

Resolutely Maria walked into the dressing room and began pinning her hair back.

"They called me," Carter said from the bedroom, speaking as if by rote. "They called me to point out that unscheduled parental appearances tend to disturb the child's adjustment."

"Adjustment to what." Maria jabbed a pin into her hair.

"We've been through this, Maria. We've done this number about fifty times."

Maria put her head in her arms on the dressing table. When she looked into the mirror again she saw Carter's reflection. There had come a time when she felt anesthetized in the presence of Ivan Costello and now that time had come with Carter.

"Don't cry," Carter said. "I know it upsets you, we're doing all we can, I said don't cry."

"I'm not crying," she said, and she was not.

10

"I'M ADAMANT about the mixes, I'm sorry, I just won't use them," the masseur who wanted to be a writer called from the kitchen. Maria lay face down on the sand beyond the sun deck and tried to neutralize, by concentrating on images of Kate (Kate's hair, brushing Kate's hair, the last time she went to the hospital Kate's hair was tangled and she had sat on the lawn and brushed it, worked out the tangles into fine golden strands, they told her not to come so often but how could she help it, they never brushed Kate's hair), the particular rise and inflection of the masseur's voice. There was always someone Maria tried not to hear at BZ and Helene's. Either there were the sulky young men BZ met in places like Acapulco and Kitzbühel and Tangier or there were Helene's friends, the women with whom she shopped and planned restorative weeks at Palm Springs and La Costa, the women with the silk Pucci shirts and the periodically tightened eye lines and the husbands on

43

perpetual location. They were always in their middle
forties, those friends of Helene's, always about ten
years older than Helene herself. "Heaven pajamas,"
Helene's friends would say to one another, and they
would exchange the addresses of new astrologers and
the tag lines of old jokes. One of Helene's friends had
been at the house when Maria and Carter arrived. "I'll
tell you one thing, he's a great *phone*," she said several times, and she and Helene would laugh. It
seemed to be a joke but Maria had failed to hear the
beginning of it. Usually Maria could avoid hearing
Helene's friends but BZ's friends were more difficult,
and this one was particularly difficult. Part of it was
his voice and part of it was that Maria had met him
before, she was certain she had. He did not seem to
recognize her but she was sure that she had met him
three years before, at someone's house in Santa Barbara. He had come in after a polo game with some
people who spoke only to the host and to one another,
never to Carter and Maria—there had been an actor
whose last several pictures had failed, the actor's
mother, and a nervous steel heiress with whom the
others seemed to have spent a week in Palm Beach—
and then he had been not a masseur but the actor's
secretary. Even lying in the noon sun on this blazing
dry October day Maria felt a physical chill when she
thought about that afternoon in Santa Barbara. The

way he looked was the problem. He looked exactly the same. He looked untouched, and she did not.

"BZ, you've planned this to torment me," he was saying now. He stood on the deck, holding a plastic lemon at elaborate arm's-length. "You couldn't possibly buy artificial lemon juice, someone left it here, it's a bad joke."

"All BZ's friends are purists," Helene murmured without opening her eyes.

"You're a nasty," BZ said, and laughed. He twisted a silver medallion on his chest so that it flashed in the sun. BZ was perpetually tanned, oiled, gleaming, not the negotiable health-club tan of people like Freddy Chaikin but tanned as evidence of a lifetime spent in season. "Isn't Helene a nasty, Carter? Haven't I got a bitch for a wife? And question number three, *who am I impersonating?*"

"Yourself," Helene suggested.

"Carter's not listening," the masseur said. "Don't be draggy, Helene, run down the beach and ask Audrey Wise for a couple of lemons. Ask Audrey and Jerry for Bloodys even. I mean we could definitely stand a few giggles."

Helene opened her eyes. "You know what Jerry gave Audrey for her birthday?"

"Let me guess." BZ touched a finger to his tongue and held it to the wind. "One perfect white rose."

"One perfect thousand-dollar bill," Helene said. "Smartass."

"Maybe she can buy herself a good fuck," BZ said.

Helene giggled. "Jerry's a good phone."

"The *lemons*," the masseur said.

Carter threw down the script he was reading and stood up. "I'll get the goddamn lemons," he said. Maria lay perfectly still until she knew that he was beyond the dunes and then she sat up, everything swimming in her vision. Beneath the faded American flag hanging over the sun deck they were arranged in tableau: BZ and the masseur, their bodies gleaming, unlined, as if they had an arrangement with mortality. Helene stood on the edge of the deck, looking down the beach toward Audrey and Jerry Wise's house. Helene was not quite so immune to time, there was a certain texture to Helene's thighs, a certain lack of resilience where fabric cut into Helene's flesh. It occurred to Maria that whatever arrangements were made, they worked less well for women. That nervous steel heiress with whom Maria had last met the masseur, something bad had happened to her. She had been shot in the face by her fourteen-year-old son. It had been in the newspapers a few years ago. After the boy killed his mother he shot himself, and was later described by his father as a victim of divorce and drugs. Maria imagined that she had sunstroke. She closed her eyes and concentrated on a prayer she had learned as a child.

"That's one less for lunch," Helene said.

"I seem to have come in after the main titles," the masseur said petulantly. "Is he going to get the lemons or isn't he?"

"Faggots make Carter nervous," Helene said pleasantly.

BZ laughed and blew Helene a kiss off his fingertips. "Actually, Nelson," he said then, "that lemon is not artificial. That lemon is re*const*ituted."

Maria stood up and grabbed a beach towel from the deck and ran into the house with the towel clutched to her mouth and a few minutes later when, pale under her sunburn and covered with cold sweat, she stopped the dry heaves and pulled off her bathing suit she saw that for the fifty-first day she was not bleeding.

11

"I WASN'T JUST CRAZY about your asking Helene how much money BZ's mother gives them to stay married," Carter said on the way back in from the beach. The top was down and Carter was driving too fast because he had to meet Freddy Chaikin and a writer from New York at Chasen's at seven o'clock. "I wasn't just crazy about that at all."

"Well, she does."

"Does what."

"Carlotta gives them money to stay married."

"So what."

"I'm sick of everybody's sick arrangements."

"You've got a fantastic vocabulary."

She looked at him and she spoke very fast and low. "I've got a fantastic vocabulary and I'm having a baby."

Carter slowed the car down. "I missed a transition," he said finally.

Maria did not look at him.

"It's not mine," he said, his voice raised. "I suppose you're going to tell me it's not mine."

"I don't know."

She did not know why she had said it but she had to. She had to get it straight. For a moment Carter said nothing.

"You don't fucking know," he said then.

She put her bare feet on the dashboard and pressed her face against her knees. Now it was a fact. He could stay or he could leave, she had set forth the fact.

"Who was it," he said.

"You know."

He kept his eyes on the highway and his foot hard on the accelerator. She wanted to tell him she was sorry, but saying she was sorry did not seem entirely adequate, and in any case what she was sorry about seemed at once too deep and too evanescent for any words she knew, seemed so vastly more complicated than the immediate fact that it was perhaps better left unraveled. The late sun glazed the Pacific. The wind burned on her face. Once they were off the Coast Highway he pulled over to the curb and stopped the car.

"I know," he said. "But Felicia doesn't."

She said nothing. It was going to be bad.

"What makes you so sure," he said then.

"I didn't say I was sure." The air seemed suddenly still and close and she pulled off her scarf. "I said I didn't know."

"I mean what makes you so sure it's happening."

"Because I went to this doctor." She spoke very fast and kept her mind on something else. It seemed to her that they had once been to dinner at somebody's house who lived off San Vicente around here, she could not remember whose house it had been but there had been Japanese food and women with long handcrafted earrings and it had been summer. "Because I went to this doctor and the test he did in his office was positive but that's not an absolutely certain test so he had me bring in some urine for a rabbit test. And he gave me this shot. And if I really wasn't the shot would make me bleed in three to five days." She paused. It came to her that in the scenario of her life this would be what was called an obligatory scene, and she wondered with distant interest just how long the scene would play. "And it was six days ago I had the shot."

"What about the test."

"What test?"

"The test you were talking about. The second test."

"The rabbit test." She was suddenly almost too exhausted to speak. "I just never called back about it."

"You were afraid to call back about it." He was

speaking in a careful monotone, a prosecutor with an open-and-shut case. "You thought if you didn't call back it would just go away."

She closed her eyes. "I guess so. I guess that's right."

"But now it's certain anyway. Otherwise the shot would have made you bleed."

She nodded mutely.

"What doctor. Who was the doctor."

"Just a doctor. On Wilshire."

"A doctor you didn't know. You thought that was smart."

She said nothing.

"I'm interested in the mechanics of this, Maria. I'm interested in how your mind works. How exactly you picked this doctor out, why this particular doctor."

Maria folded her scarf and smoothed it carefully over her bare knees. "He was near Saks," she whispered finally. "I was having my hair done at Saks."

12

LATE THAT NIGHT sitting alone in the dark by the pool she remembered whose house it had been out off San Vicente with the Japanese food, it had been the house of a couple named Sidney and Ruth Loomis. Sidney Loomis was a television writer and Ruth Loomis was very active in the civil-rights movement and group therapy. Maria had never been able to think of anything to say to Ruth Loomis, but in retrospect that was not why Carter had stopped seeing Sidney and Ruth Loomis. He had stopped seeing them because the show Sidney Loomis was writing had been canceled in midseason and he did not pick up another. Maria tried very hard to keep thinking of Carter in this light, Carter as a dropper of friends and names and obligations, because if she thought of Carter as he was tonight she would begin to cry again. He had left the house. He had neither met Freddy Chaikin at Chasen's nor called to say that he was not coming. She knew that because Freddy Chaikin had called for him. She had at last done something that reached him, but now it was too late. "What am I supposed to do," he had said before he left the house. "What in fuck am I supposed to do?"

13

WHEN CARTER CALLED the next morning it was from the motel on the desert. His voice was measured, uninflected, as if he had been saying the words to himself all night. "I love you," she whispered, but it was more a plea than a declaration and in any case he made no response. "Get a pencil," he ordered. He was going to give her a telephone number. He was going to give her the telephone number of the only man in Los Angeles County who did clean work.

"Then we'll see."

"I'm not sure I want to do that," she said carefully.

"All right, don't do it. Go ahead and have this kid." He paused, confident in his hand. She waited for him to play it through. "And I'll take Kate."

After he hung up she sat very still. She had a remote sense that everything was happening exactly the way it was supposed to happen. By the time she called him back she was calm, neutral, an intermediary calling to clarify the terms. "Listen," she said. "If I do this, then you promise I can have Kate? You promise there won't be trouble later?"

"I'm not promising anything," he said. "I said we'll see."

14

AT FOUR THAT AFTERNOON, after a day spent looking at the telephone and lighting cigarettes and putting the cigarettes out and getting glasses of water and looking at the telephone again, Maria dialed the number. A man answered, and said that he would call back. When he did he asked who had referred her.

"You want an appointment with the doctor," he said.

"When could he see me."

"The doctor will want to know how many weeks."

"How many weeks what?"

There was a silence. "How advanced is the *problem*, Maria," the voice said finally.

15

"THE FOOD WAS UNSPEAKABLE, my clothes mildewed in the closet, you can *have* Cozumel," BZ's mother said. She was playing solitaire and Maria sat transfixed by the light striking off the diamond bracelets on her thin tanned wrists. "Also Machu Picchu," she added, slapping down another card.

"I can't even dream whÿ you stopped at Cozumel," Helene said. "I mean since you can't bear Mexicans."

"BZ said it was marvelous, that's why."

"BZ likes Mexicans."

"I know why BZ likes Mexicans." Carlotta Mendenhall Fisher shuffled the cards once and pointed at Maria. "Did you ask this child for dinner?" she demanded. "Or didn't you?"

"It's just seven, Carlotta. I thought we'd have another drink."

"I always serve at seven."

"The last time I was in Pebble Beach," Helene said, "you served at quarter to eleven."

Helene and her mother-in-law looked at each other for an instant and then Carlotta began to laugh. "This girl is my own natural child," she said finally to Maria, gasping through her laughter. "The daughter I didn't have."

"Speaking of the one you did have," Helene said, "does Nikki know you're back in the country?"

"*Nikki.* Nikki's like this child, I bore her." She looked at Maria. "Don't I bore you. Admit it."

Maria looked up uncertainly. The voice on the telephone had known what she wanted without either of them saying it. The voice on the telephone had said that this would be expensive. The voice on the telephone had told her that on the day set she was to bring a pad and a belt and $1,000 in cash. In confusion Maria looked away from Carlotta's bright blue eyes, glittering like her bracelets.

"Isn't it kind of . . ." Maria trailed off.

"Isn't *what?*"

"I mean Cozumel," Maria said finally. "Isn't it the off season."

"Of *course* the off season," Carlotta said triumphantly.

The voice had called her Maria.

The voice had said that he would be in touch.

"Carlotta's a demon for thrift," Helene said.

"Now what about my boring you," Carlotta said.

16

THE NEXT MORNING in the dry still heat she woke crying for her mother. She had not cried for her mother since the bad season in New York, the season when she had done nothing but walk and cry and lose so much weight that the agency refused to book her. She had not been able to eat that year because every time she looked at food the food would seem to arrange itself into ominous coils. She had known that there was no rattlesnake on her plate but once the image had seized her there was no eating the food. She was consumed that year by questions. Exactly what time had it happened, precisely what had she been doing in New York at the instant her mother lost control of the car outside Tonopah. What was her mother wearing, thinking. What was she doing in Tonopah anyway. She imagined her mother having a doctor's appointment in Tonopah, and the doctor saying cancer, and her mother cracking up the car on purpose. She imagined her mother trying to call her from a pay phone in Tonopah, standing in a booth with all her quarters and dimes and nickels spread on the shelf and getting the operator and getting New York and then the answering service picking up the call. Maria did not know whether any of that had actually happened but she used to think it, used to think it particularly around the time the sun set in New York, think about the mother dying in the desert light, the daughter unavailable in the Eastern dark. She would imagine the quarters and dimes and nickels spread out on the shelf and the light in the cottonwoods and she would wonder what she was doing in the dark. What time is it there, her mother would have asked had she gotten Maria. What's the weather. She might never have said what was on her mind but she would have left a coded message, said goodbye. One time Maria had saved enough money to give her mother a trip around the world, but instead she had lent the money to Ivan Costello, and then her mother was dead.

"I'm not crying," Maria said when Carter called from the desert at 8 a.m. "I'm perfectly all right."

"You don't sound perfectly all right."

"I had a bad dream."

There was a silence. "You called the doctor?"

"Yes. I called the doctor." She spoke very rapidly

and distantly. "Everything's arranged. Everything's perfectly taken care of."

"What did—"

"I have to go now. I have to hang up. I have to see somebody about a job."

"Just hold on a minute, Maria, I want to know what the doctor said."

She was staring into a hand mirror, picking out her mother's features. Sometime in the night she had moved into a realm of miseries peculiar to women, and she had nothing to say to Carter.

"I said what did they *say*, Maria."

"They said they'd call me up some day and on the day they called me up I'd meet them some place with a pad and a belt and $1,000 in cash. All right, Carter? All right?"

17

ALTHOUGH THE HEAT had not yet broken she began that week to sleep inside, between white sheets, hoping dimly that the white sheets would effect some charm, that she would wake in the morning and find them stained with blood. She did this in the same spirit that she had, a month before, thrown a full box of Tampax into the garbage: to be without Tampax was to insure bleeding, to sleep naked between white sheets was to guarantee staining. To give the charm every opportunity she changed the immaculate sheets every morning. She wore white crêpe pajamas and no underwear to a party. She pretended to herself that she was keeping the baby, the better to invite disappointment, court miscarriage. "I'm having a baby," she heard herself telling the parking-lot attendant at Saks as they tried vainly to get a wicker bassinette into the Corvette. When it became clear that she would have to leave the bassinette for delivery she sat in the driver's seat of the Corvette and cried. She was crying too much. All the time now, when she was driving and when she was trying to clean a bathroom and when she was pretending to herself that she could have the baby, she was wondering where and when it was going to happen.

"Any calls," she asked the service.

"Mr. Goodwin, New York, three times, you're to call immediately."

She looked again into the hand mirror and again saw her mother. "Tell him I haven't picked up my messages." She had nothing to say to any of them.

18

"Monday," the voice on the telephone said. "Monday at five o'clock. We'll be in touch again on Monday."

"Where," she said. "Where do I go."

"I said we'll be in touch, Maria. We will."

She drove to the beach, but there was oil scum on the sand and a red tide in the flaccid surf and mounds of kelp at the waterline. The kelp hummed with flies. The water lapped warm, forceless. When she got back into town she drove aimlessly down Sunset, pulled into a drive-in at the corner of La Brea, and, briefly flushed into purposefulness by a Coca-Cola, walked barefoot across the hot asphalt to a telephone booth.

"This is Maria," she said helplessly when Felicia Goodwin picked up the telephone in New York. She did not know why but she had not counted on talking to Felicia. "I just wondered when you were coming back."

"We've been trying to get you for *days*." Felicia always spoke on the telephone as if a spurious urgency could mask her radical lack of interest in talking to anyone. Sometimes Maria was depressed by how much she and Felicia had in common. "Les was worried something had happened to you, I said no, she's on the desert with Carter—didn't you call the service?"

"Not exactly."

"Anyway we'll be out in a few days, this time to stay, we're going to buy a house—" Felicia's voice faded, as if she had stretched her capacity for communication to its limit.

"Les finished the script?"

"I'll get him," Felicia said with relief.

"Never mind," Maria said, but it was too late.

"Where've you been," he said.

"Nowhere." When she heard his voice she felt a rush of well-being. "I didn't want to call because—"

"I can't hear you, Maria, where are you?"

"In a phone booth. I just wanted—"

"You all right?"

"No. I mean yes." A bus was shifting gears on Sunset and she raised her voice. "Listen. Call me."

She walked back to the car and sat for a long while in the parking lot, idling the engine and watching a woman in a muumuu walk out of the Carolina Pines

Motel and cross the street to a supermarket. The woman walked in small mincing steps and kept raising her hand to shield her eyes from the vacant sunlight. As if in trance Maria watched the woman, for it seemed to her then that she was watching the dead still center of the world, the quintessential intersection of nothing. She did not know why she had told Les Goodwin to call her.

19

"You want it in cash," the teller said doubtfully.

"I'm taking a trip." She did not know why she was saying this but she kept on. "Mexico City, Guadalajara."

"You don't want traveler's checks?"

"*Cash*," she said, and when the teller handed her the bills she ran from the bank with them still in her hand.

In the car she counted the stiff bills. They stuck together and she missed one and she counted them four more times before she was certain she had them all. Since early morning she had been trying to remember something Les Goodwin had said to her, anything Les Goodwin had said to her. When she was not actually talking to him now she found it hard to keep him distinct from everyone else, everyone with whom she had ever slept or almost slept or refused to sleep or wanted to sleep. It had seemed this past month as if they were all one, that her life had been a single sexual encounter, one dreamed fuck, no beginnings or endings, no point beyond itself. She tried to remember how it had been to drag Fremont Street in Vegas with Earl Lee Atkins when she was sixteen years old, how it had been to go out on the desert between Vegas and Boulder and drink beer from half-quart cans and feel her sunburn when he touched her and smell the chlorine from her own hair and the Lava soap from his and the sweet sharp smell of starched cotton soaked with sweat. *How High the Moon,* the radio would play, Les Paul and Mary Ford. She tried to remember Ivan Costello, tried to fix in her mind the exact way the light came through the shutters in his bedroom in New York, the exact colors of the striped sheets she had put on his bed and the way those sheets looked in the morning and the look of a motel room in which they had once spent a week in Maryland. She tried to remember Carter. She tried to remember Les Goodwin. She could remember it all but none of it seemed to come to anything. She had a sense the dream had ended and she had slept on.

20

"Nothing's wrong," she repeated to Les Goodwin on the telephone.

"I know something's wrong."

"Nothing."

"O.K.," he said finally. "All right. I'm coming out alone on Monday, meet my plane at four."

"I can't."

"I want to *talk* to you, Maria. I want to see you."

"Monday night," she said. "Listen. You make me happy."

She hung up very fast then because she did not want to find herself telling him why she could not meet his flight.

21

In the dream from which she woke when the telephone rang again that night she had the baby, and she and the baby and Kate were living on West Twelfth Street with Ivan Costello. In the dream she did not yet know Carter, but somehow had Carter's daughter and Carter's blessing. In the dream it was all right. She supposed that she had dreamed of Ivan Costello because the telephone was ringing, and he used to call her in the middle of the night. "How much do you want it," he used to say. "Tell me what you'd do to get it from me." The telephone was still ringing and she pulled the cord loose from the jack. She could not remember what she would have done to get it from any of them.

22

"You should always call before you come," the nurse in charge of Kate's cottage said on Sunday. The nurse had short hair and a faint moustache and Kate clung to her knees and Maria did not like her. "The new medication, new treatment, naturally she's not—"

"What new medication," Maria heard herself saying. "You keep talking about the new medication, I mean *what is it.*"

Kate screamed. The nurse looked reproachfully at Maria. "Methylphenidate hydrochloride."

Maria closed her eyes. "All right. Your point."

"We definitely would have suggested you wait until next week."

"I won't be here next week."

"You're going away?"

"Cozumel," Maria said. "Mexico."

On the way to the parking lot she twice invented pretexts to run back, kiss Kate's small fat hands, tell her to be good. The third time she ran back it was to find the nurse.

"One thing. You know when she wakes up at night and says '*oise, oise,*' it means she's . . ." Maria faltered. She realized that she expected to die. All along she had expected to die, as surely as she expected that planes would crash if she boarded them in bad spirit, as unquestionably as she believed that loveless marriage ended in cancer of the cervix and equivocal adultery in fatal accidents to children. Maria did not particularly believe in rewards, only in punishments, swift and personal. "It means she's having a nightmare," she said finally.

The nurse looked at her impassively.

"I mean I don't know if I ever told you that."

"I'm sure you did," the nurse said.

That night the house crackled with malign electricity. A hot wind came up at midnight and the leaves scraped the screens, a loose storm drain slapped against the roof. Sometime in the night Maria wrote three letters which, before dawn, she tore up and flushed down the toilet. The bits of paper kept floating back into the toilet bowl and by the time she finally got rid of them it was light, and all the daisies in the garden had been snapped by the wind, and the concrete around the swimming pool was littered with fallen palm fronds. At six-thirty that morning she placed a call to Carter at the motel on the desert but Carter had already left for the location. She interpreted that as a sign and did not try to call the location. She would do what he wanted. She would do this one last thing and then they would never be able to touch her again.

23

SHE TRIED TO STRAIGHTEN a drawer, and abandoned it. She heard fire reports on the radio, and turned the sprinklers on the ivy. For almost two hours she studied an old issue of *Vogue* she picked up in the poolhouse, her attention fixed particularly on the details of the life led in New York and Rome by the wife of an Italian industrialist. The Italian seemed to find a great deal of purpose in her life, seemed to make decisions and stick by them, and Maria studied the photographs as if a key might be found among them. When she had exhausted the copy of *Vogue* she got out her checkbook and a stack of bills and spread them on the kitchen table. Paying bills sometimes lent her the illusion of order but now each bill she opened seemed fresh testimony to her life's disorder, its waste and diffusion: flowers sent to people whom she had failed to thank for parties, sheets bought for beds in which no one now slept, an old bill from F.A.O. Schwarz for a tricycle Kate had never ridden. When she wrote out the check to Schwarz her hand trembled so hard that she had to void the first check, and smoke a cigarette before she could write another.

"Get it right, Maria," the voice on the telephone said. "You got a pencil there? You writing this down?"

"Yes," Maria said.

"Ventura Freeway north, you got that all right? You know what exit?"

"I wrote it down."

"All set, then. I'll meet you in the parking lot of the Thriftimart."

"What Thriftimart," Maria whispered.

"Maria, I told you, you can't miss it. Under the big red T."

In the aftermath of the wind the air was dry, burning, so clear that she could see the ploughed furrows of firebreaks on distant mountains. Not even the highest palms moved. The stillness and clarity of the air seemed to rob everything of its perspective, seemed to alter all perception of depth, and Maria drove as carefully as if she were reconnoitering an atmosphere without gravity. Taco Bells jumped out at her. Oil rockers creaked ominously. For miles before she reached the Thriftimart she could see the big red T, a forty-foot cutout letter which seemed peculiarly illuminated against the harsh unclouded light of the afternoon sky.

24

"YOU DRIVE," the man had said. "We'll pick up my car after."

He was wearing white duck pants and a white sport shirt and he had a moon face and a eunuch's soft body. The hand resting on his knee was pale and freckled and boneless and ever since he got in the car he had been humming *I Get a Kick Out of You.*

"You familiar with this area, Maria?"

The question seemed obscurely freighted. "No," Maria said finally.

"Nice homes here. Nice for kids." The voice was bland, ingratiating, the voice on the telephone. "Let me ask you one question, all right?"

Maria nodded, and tightened her grip on the steering wheel.

"Get pretty good mileage on this? Or no?"

"Pretty good," she heard herself saying after only the slightest pause. "Not too bad."

"You may have noticed, I drive a Cadillac. Eldorado. Eats gas but I like it, like the feel of it."

Maria said nothing. That, then, had actually been the question. She had not misunderstood.

"If I decided to get rid of the Cad," he said, "I might pick myself up a little Camaro. Maybe that sounds like a step down, a Cad to a Camaro, but I've got my eye on this particular Camaro, exact model of the pace car in the Indianapolis 500."

"You think you'll buy a Camaro," Maria said in the neutral tone of a therapist.

"Get the right price, I just might. I got a friend, he can write me a sweet deal if it's on the floor much longer. They almost had a buyer last week but lucky for me—here, Maria, right here, pull into this driveway."

Maria turned off the ignition and looked at the man in the white duck pants with an intense and grateful interest. In the past few minutes he had significantly altered her perception of reality: she saw now that she was not a woman on her way to have an abortion. She was a woman parking a Corvette outside a tract house while a man in white pants talked about buying a Camaro. There was no more to it than that. "Lucky for you what?"

"Lucky for me, the guy's credit didn't hold up."

25

THE FLOOR OF THE BEDROOM where it happened was covered with newspapers. She remembered reading somewhere that newspapers were antiseptic, it had to do with the chemicals in the ink, to deliver a baby in a farmhouse you covered the floor with newspapers. There was something else to be done with newspapers, something unexpected, some emergency trick: quilts could be made with newspapers. In time of disaster you could baste newspapers to both sides of a cotton blanket and end up with a warm quilt. She knew a lot of things about disaster. She could manage. Carter could never manage but she could. She could not think where she had learned all these tricks. Probably in her mother's *American Red Cross Handbook,* gray with a red cross on the cover. There, that was a good thing to think about, at any rate not a bad thing if she kept her father out of it. If she could concentrate for even one minute on a picture of herself as a ten-year-old sitting on the front steps of the house in Silver Wells reading the gray book with the red cross on the cover (splints, shock, rattlesnake bite, rattlesnake bite was why her mother made her read it) with the heat shimmering off the corrugated tin roof of the shed across the road (her father was not in this picture, keep him out of it, say he had gone into Vegas with Benny Austin), if she could concentrate for one more minute on that shed, on whether this minute twenty years later the heat still shimmered off its roof, those were two minutes during which she was not entirely party to what was happening in this bedroom in Encino.

Two minutes in Silver Wells, two minutes here, two minutes there, it was going to be over in this bedroom in Encino, it could not last forever. The walls of the bedroom were cream-colored, yellow, a wallpaper with a modest pattern. Whoever had chosen that wallpaper would have liked maple furniture, a maple bedroom set, a white chenille bedspread and a white Princess telephone, all gone now but she could see it as it must have been, could see even the woman who had picked the wallpaper, she would be a purchaser of Audubon prints and scented douches, a hoarder of secret sexual grievances, a wife. Two minutes in Silver Wells, two minutes on the wallpaper, it could not last forever. The table was a doctor's table but not fitted with stirrups: instead there were two hardbacked chairs with pillows tied over the backs. "Tell me if it's too cold," the doctor said. The doctor was tall and haggard and wore a rubber apron. "Tell me now because I won't be able to touch the air conditioner once I start."

She said that it was not too cold.

"No, it's too cold. You don't weigh enough, it's too cold."

He adjusted the dial but the sound remained level. She closed her eyes and tried to concentrate on the sound. Carter did not like air conditioners but there had been one somewhere. She had slept in a room with an air conditioner, the question was where, never mind the question, that question led nowhere. "This is just induced menstruation," she could hear the doctor saying. "Nothing to have any emotional difficulties about, better not to think about it at all, quite often the pain is worse when we think about it, don't like anesthetics, anesthetics are where we run into trouble, just a little local on the cervix, there, relax, Maria, I said *relax*."

No moment more or less important than any other moment, all the same: the pain as the doctor scraped signified nothing beyond itself, no more constituted the pattern of her life than did the movie on television in the living room of this house in Encino. The man in the white duck pants was sitting out there watching the movie and she was lying in here not watching the movie, and that was all there was to that. Why the volume on the set was turned up so high seemed another question better left unasked. "Hear that scraping, Maria?" the doctor said. "That should be the sound of music to you . . . don't scream, Maria, there are people next door, almost done, almost over, better to get it all now than do it again a month from now . . . I said don't make any noise, Maria, now I'll tell you what's going to happen, you'll bleed a day or so, not heavily, just spotting, and then a month, six weeks from now you'll have a normal period, not this month, this month you just had it, it's in that pail."

He went into the bathroom then (later she would try to fix in her mind the exact circumstances of his leaving the bedroom, would try to remember if he took the pail with him, later that would seem important to her) and by the time he came back the contractions had stopped. He gave her one envelope of tetracycline capsules and another of ergot tablets and by six o'clock of that hot October afternoon she was out of the bedroom in Encino and back in the car with the man in the white duck pants. The late sun seemed warm and benevolent on her skin and everything she saw looked beautiful, the summer pulse of life itself made manifest. As she backed out of the driveway she smiled radiantly at her companion.

"You missed a pretty fair movie," he said. "Paula Raymond." He reached into his pocket for what seemed to be a cigarette holder. "Ever since I gave up smoking I carry these by the dozen, they look like regular holders but all you get is air."

Maria stared at his outstretched hand.

"*Take* it. I noticed you're still smoking. You'll thank me some day."

"Thank you."

"I'm a regular missionary." The man in the white duck pants resettled his soft bulk and gazed out the car window. "Gee, Paula Raymond was a pretty girl," he said then. "Funny she never became a star."

26

"I WANT A VERY LARGE STEAK," she said to Les Goodwin in a restaurant on Melrose at eight o'clock that night. "And before the very large steak I want three drinks. And after the steak I want to go somewhere with very loud music."

"Like where."

"I don't know where. You ought to know *where*. You know a lot of places with loud music."

"What's the matter with you."

"I am just very very very tired of listening to you all."

27

SILVER WELLS was with her again. She wanted to see her mother. She wanted to go back to the last day she had spent with her mother: a Sunday. She had flown out from New York on Friday and then it was Sunday and Benny Austin was there for Sunday dinner and after dinner they would all drive down to Vegas to put Maria back on the airplane.

"Your mom's O.K., don't worry about your mom," Benny muttered when he and Maria were alone for a moment at the table. "Believe me it's nothing."

"What's nothing? What's the matter with her?"

"Nothing on God's earth, Maria, that's what I'm telling you. You might say she's a little depressed, naturally your father doesn't want to talk about it."

"Depressed," Maria repeated.

"Nothing, Maria, believe me. Here they come, we're talking about the zinc boom." Benny cleared his throat. "I've been telling Maria about the zinc boom, Harry."

"You into zinc?" Maria said finally. She was watching her mother but her mother looked just as she always had.

"We've been buying a few rights." Harry Wyeth began whistling through his teeth.

"Meal fit for the Queen of Spain," Benny said. "Francine, you could make a fortune in the take-out spare-rib business."

Francine Wyeth laughed. "Maria and I can always open a hash house. When we get sick of you all."

"Hash house on 95," Harry Wyeth said. "Pretty picture."

"*Not* on 95," Francine Wyeth said. "*Somewhere else.*"

Maria closed her eyes.

"I'm talking about a quantity operation. Franchises, you rent out your name and your receipt." Benny Austin talked as if nothing had happened at the table. "Franchised services, that's where the future lies."

"I don't want to go back," Maria said.

"That's natural." Harry Wyeth did not look at his wife or daughter. "That's only natural. Don't think about it, you'll be out again in a month or two, plan on it now."

"She's too thin," Francine Wyeth said. "Look at her, see for yourself."

"She can't win if she's not at the table, Francine."

Harry Wyeth threw down his napkin and stood up. "You wouldn't understand.that."

That night as the plane taxied out onto the runway at McCarran Maria had kept her face pressed against the window for as long as she could see them, her mother and father and Benny Austin, waving at the wrong window.

28

"Helene's going up to Pebble Beach to spend the weekend with BZ's mother," Carter said when he called from the desert. "Why don't you fly up and meet her there."

"I can't."

"Too busy, I suppose."

Maria said nothing.

"Or maybe you're afraid you might have a good time."

"I said I *can't*."

"Why can't you, just for the record."

"She's not my mother," Maria said.

29

THE BLEEDING BEGAN a few weeks later. "It's nothing," the doctor on Wilshire said when she finally went. "Whoever did it did all right. It's clean, no infection, count your blessings."

"The pain."

"You're just menstruating early, I'll give you some Edrisal."

The Edrisal did not work and neither did some Darvon she found in the bathroom and she slept that night with a gin bottle by her bed. She did not think she was menstruating. She wanted to talk to her mother.

30

"I'VE GOT NEWS," Freddy Chaikin said after the waiter had brought her Bloody Mary and his Perrier water. "I didn't want to break it until it was set. Morty Landau, I predicted it, he's in love with you. You've got a guest-star on a two-part *Interstate 80*."

"That's fine, Freddy." She tried for more conviction. "That's really fine."

He watched her drain her glass. "It'll get you seen."

"Actually I'm not feeling too well."

"You mean you don't want to work."

"I didn't say that. I just said I wasn't feeling too well."

"Maria, I empathize. What you and Carter are going through, it tears my heart out. Believe me, I've been through it. Which is why I know that *work is the best medicine for things wrong in the private-life department*. And I don't want to sound like an agent, but ten percent of nothing doesn't pay the bar bill." He laughed, and then looked at her. "A joke, Maria. Just a joke."

31

THE BLEEDING CAME AND WENT and came again. By late afternoon of her third day's work on *Interstate 80* there were involuntary pain lines on her forehead and she could not stand entirely upright for more than a few seconds. She sat back in the shadows on the edge of the set and prayed that the cameramen would be so slow with the set-ups that the day's last shot would be delayed until morning. At five-thirty they got the shot in three takes and later in the parking lot she could not remember doing it.

By midnight the blood was coming so fast that she soaked three pads in fifteen minutes. There was blood on the bed, blood on the floor, blood on the bathroom tiles. She thought about calling Les Goodwin—it would be all right to call him, she knew that Felicia was in San Francisco—but she did not. She called Carter.

"Get the doctor," Carter said.

"I don't exactly want to do that."

"For Christ's sake then get to an emergency hospital."

"I can't," she said finally. "The thing is, I'm working tomorrow."

"What do you mean, *work*ing. What in fuck does *work*ing mean. You just told me you were *dying*."

"I never said that."

"You said you were afraid."

Maria said nothing.

"Jesus Christ, Maria, I'm out here on the desert, I can't do anything, will you please get to a hospital or do you want me to call the police to come *get* you."

"You just want me in a hospital so that nothing'll happen to make you feel guilty," she said then, said it before she meant to speak, and when she heard the words she broke out in a sweat. "*Listen*," she said. "I didn't mean that. I'm just tired. Listen. I'll call the doctor right now."

"You have to swear to me." Carter's voice was drained, exhausted. "You have to swear you'll call the doctor. And call me back if something's wrong."

"I promise."

Instead she took a Dexedrine to stay awake. Awake she could always call an ambulance. Awake she could save herself if it came to that. In the morning, from the studio, she called the doctor.

"I'll meet you at St. John's," he said.

"I can't go to the hospital. I told you before, I'm working."

"You're hemorrhaging, you can't work."

"Oh yes I can work," she said, and hung up. She had wanted to ask him for more Dexedrine, but instead she got some from a hairdresser on the set. While she was changing she found a large piece of bloodied tissue on the pad she had been wearing, and she put it in an envelope and dropped it by the doctor's office on her way home from the studio. When she called the next day the doctor said that the tissue was part of the placenta, and that was the end of that. For the first time in two weeks she slept through the night, and was an hour late for her morning call.

32

"You were going to come over and use the sauna," Larry Kulik said.

"I've been—"

"So I hear."

"Hear what."

"Hear you're ready for a nuthouse, you want to know."

"You think I need a sauna."

"I think you need something."

Maria said nothing.

"I'm a good friend to people I like," Larry Kulik said. "Think it over."

33

A FEW DAYS LATER the dreams began. She was in touch with a member of a shadowy Syndicate. Sometimes the contact was Freddy Chaikin, sometimes an F.B.I. man she had met once in New York and not thought of since. Certain phrases remained constant. Always he explained that he was "part of that operation." Always he wanted to discuss "a business proposition." Always he mentioned a plan to use the house in Beverly Hills for "purposes which would in no way concern" her. She need only supply certain information: the condition of the plumbing, the precise width of the pipes, the location and size of all the clean-outs. Workmen appeared, rooms were prepared. The man in the white duck pants materialized and then the doctor, in his rubber apron. At that point she would fight for consciousness but she was never able to wake herself before the dream revealed its inexorable intention, before the plumbing stopped up, before they all fled and left her there, gray water bubbling up in every sink. Of course she could not call a plumber, because she had known all along what would be found in the pipes, what hacked pieces of human flesh.

34

IN NOVEMBER THE HEAT BROKE, and Carter went to New York to cut the picture, and Maria still had the dream. On the morning a sink backed up in the house in Beverly Hills she looked in the classified for another place to sleep.

"You'd be surprised the history this place has," the man said as he showed her the apartment. He was wearing a pumpkin velour beach robe and wrap-around glasses and she had found him not in the apartment marked "Mgr." but out on Fountain Avenue, hosing down the sidewalk. "As a writer, it might interest you to know that Philip Dunne once had 2-D."

"I'm not a writer," Maria said.

"Excuse me, it was Sidney Howard." He took off his glasses and wiped them on a sleeve of the beach robe. "Or so the legend goes."

In December the Christmas tree on top of the Capitol Records Tower came and went, and Maria had Kate for three days. They drove up and down La Brea looking for a Christmas tree and had Christmas dinner at Les and Felicia Goodwin's new house and Kate smashed the Victorian doll Felicia had given her against a large mirror.

"She misses Carter," Felicia murmured, distraught beyond the immediate breakage.

"You don't know what the fuck you're talking about," Les Goodwin said.

Kate's eyes darted from Maria to Les to Felicia and back to Maria and then, preternaturally attuned to the threat of voices not even raised, she began to scream. The mother apologizing, the child screaming, the polished floor covered with shards of broken mirror and flesh-colored ceramic, they left the Christmas dinner. All that night the two of them held each other with a dumb protective ferocity but the next day at the hospital, parting, only Maria cried.

In January there were poinsettias in front of all the bungalows between Melrose and Sunset, and the rain set in, and Maria wore not sandals but real shoes and a Shetland sweater she had bought in New York the year she was nineteen. For days during the rain she did not speak out loud or read a newspaper. She could not read newspapers because certain stories leapt at her from the page: the four-year-olds in the abandoned refrigerator, the tea party with Purex, the infant in the driveway, rattlesnake in the playpen, the peril, unspeakable peril, in the everyday. She grew faint as the processions swept before her, the children alive when last scolded, dead when next seen, the children in the locked car burning, the little faces, helpless screams. The mothers were always reported to be under sedation. In the whole world there was not as much sedation as there was instantaneous peril. Maria ate frozen enchiladas, looked at television for word of the world, thought of herself as under sedation and did not leave the apartment on Fountain Avenue.

35

"I DON'T KNOW if you noticed, I'm mentally ill," the woman said. The woman was sitting next to Maria at the snack counter in Ralph's Market. "I'm *talking* to you."

Maria turned around. "I'm sorry."

"I've been mentally ill for seven years. You don't know what a struggle it is to get through a day like this."

"This is a bad day for you," Maria said in a neutral voice.

"What's so different about this day."

Maria looked covertly at the pay phones but there was still a line. The telephone in the apartment was out of order and she had to report it. The line at the pay phones in Ralph's Market suddenly suggested to Maria a disorganization so general that the norm was to have either a disconnected telephone or some clandestine business to conduct, some extramarital error. She had to have a telephone. There was no one to whom she wanted to talk but she had to have a telephone. If she could not be reached it would happen, the peril would find Kate. Beside her the woman's voice rose and fell monotonously.

"I mean you can't fathom the despair. Believe me I've thought of ending it. Kaput. Over. Head in the oven."

"A doctor," Maria said.

"*Doctor*. I've talked to doctors."

"You'll feel better. Try to feel better." The girl now using the nearest telephone seemed to be calling a taxi to take her home from Ralph's. The girl had rollers in her hair and a small child in her basket and Maria wondered whether her car had been repossessed or her husband had left her or just what had happened, why was she calling a taxi from Ralph's. "I mean you have to try, you can't feel this way forever."

"I'll say I can't." Tears began to roll down the woman's face. "You don't even want to talk to me."

"But I do." Maria touched her arm. "I do."

"*Get your whore's hands off me,*" the woman screamed.

36

"THERE'S SOME PRINCIPLE I'm not grasping, Maria," Carter said on the telephone from New York. "You've got a $1,500-a-month house sitting empty in Beverly Hills, and you're living in a furnished apartment on Fountain Avenue. You want to be closer to Schwab's? Is that it?"

Maria lay on the bed watching a television news film of a house about to slide into the Tujunga Wash. "I'm not living here, I'm just staying here."

"I still don't get the joke."

She kept her eyes on the screen. "Then don't get it," she said at the exact instant the house splintered and fell.

After Carter had hung up Maria wrapped her robe close and smoked part of a joint and watched an interview with the woman whose house it had been. "You boys did a really outstanding camera job," the woman said. Maria finished the cigarette and repeated the compliment out loud. The day's slide and flood news was followed by a report of a small earth tremor centered near Joshua Tree, 4.2 on the Richter Scale, and, of corollary interest, an interview with a Pentecostal minister who had received prophecy that eight million people would perish by earthquake on a Friday afternoon in March. The notion of general devastation had for Maria a certain sedative effect (the rattlesnake in the playpen, that was different, that was particular, that was punitive), suggested an instant in which all anxieties would be abruptly gratified, and between the earthquake prophecy and the marijuana and the cheerful detachment of the woman whose house was in the Tujunga Wash, she felt a kind of resigned tranquillity. Within these four rented walls she was safe. She was more than safe, she was all right: she had seen herself on *Interstate 80* just before the news and she looked all right. Warm, content, suffused with tentative small resolves, Maria fell asleep before the news was over.

But the next morning when the shower seemed slow to drain she threw up in the toilet, and after she had stopped trembling packed the few things she had brought to Fountain Avenue and, in the driving rain, drove back to the house in Beverly Hills. There would be plumbing anywhere she went.

37

"I'm going to do it," she would say on the telephone.

"Then do it," Carter would say. "It's better."

"You think it's better."

"If it's what you want."

"What do *you* want."

"It's never been right," he would say. "It's been shit."

"I'm sorry."

"I know you're sorry. I'm sorry."

"We could try," one or the other would say after a while.

"We've already tried," the other would say.

By the time Carter came back to town in February the dialogue was drained of energy, the marriage lanced.

"I've got a new lawyer," she told him. "You can use Steiner."

"I'll call him today."

"I'll need a witness."

"Helene," he said. "Helene can do it." He seemed relieved that the dialogue had worn itself down to legal details, satisfied that he could offer Helene. He would be staying in BZ and Helene's guest house while they were looping and scoring the picture. He would speak to Helene immediately. Maria felt herself a sleepwalker to the courthouse.

"Let's see . . . an afternoon hearing." Helene spaced the words as if she were consulting an engagement book. "That means lunch before instead of after."

"We don't have to have lunch."

"Day of days, Maria. Of course lunch."

On the day of the hearing Maria overslept, thick with Seconal. When she walked into the Bistro half an hour late for lunch she could only think dimly how healthy Helene looked, how suntanned and somehow invincible with her silk shirt and tinted glasses and long streaked hair and a new square emerald that covered one of her fingers to the knuckle.

"Straighten your shoulders," Helene said, lifting her drink slightly as Maria sat down. "You look spectral. We should go to the Springs together." Helene's eyes were not on Maria but on two women who sat across the room. "Allene Walsh has a new *friend*," she murmured to Maria as she smiled at the older of the two women. "They've been spooning food into each other's mouths for the past half hour."

"She's an actress named Sharon Carrol, I worked with her once." Maria tried to summon up some other detail to assuage Helene's avid interest in other people. "She kept a dildo in her dressing room."

"Allene Walsh has more dildoes around her house than anybody I ever knew. Look at my new ring."

"I saw it."

"From Carlotta." Helene studied the emerald. "For staying on the desert. Speaking of *new friends*. I mean he was shuttling them in and out of that motel like the dailies, I couldn't even get up for a Nembutal without knocking over somebody's bottle of *Monsieur Y.*" For an instant Helene's face seemed to lose its animation, and when she spoke again her voice was flat and preoccupied. "You look like hell, Maria, this isn't any excuse for you to fall apart, I mean a *divorce*. I've done it twice."

"I thought only once."

"Twice," Helene said without interest. "BZ says once because that's what he told his mother." She was intent upon her reflection in the mirror behind the table, tracing a line with one finger from her chin to her temple. "You can really tell," she said finally.

"Tell what?"

"Tell I haven't done my Laszlo in three days."

Helene's voice was still flat but her interest seemed revived.

At two o'clock they met Carter and the lawyers outside the courtroom in Santa Monica, and at two-thirty Maria swore and Helene confirmed that the defendant, Carter Lang, had repeatedly struck and in other ways humiliated the plaintiff, Mrs. Maria Lang. The charge was mental cruelty, uncontested. This Mrs. Maria Lang to whom the lawyers referred seemed to Maria someone other than herself, an aggrieved wife she might see interviewed on television. As they waited for the details to be cleared up, the papers to be signed, Maria sat very still with her hands in her lap. Helene stirred restlessly beside her, her eyes across the aisle, on Carter and his lawyer. "*Carter,*" Helene whispered finally, leaning across Maria to attract his attention. "*Puzzle of the week. Guess which two dykes were seen feeding each other cheese soufflé in the Bistro today.*"

38

"WHAT HAVE YOU BEEN DOING," Carter said the next time she saw him.

"Working. I'm going to be working very soon."

"I mean who've you been seeing."

"Nobody. Helene. BZ. BZ comes by sometimes."

"Don't get into that," Carter said.

"He's your friend," Maria said.

39

THE FIRST TIME Maria ever met BZ it had been at the beach house and it had been two o'clock on a weekday afternoon and it was the summer Carter was cutting *Angel Beach*.

"I've got a meeting at the beach with this guy from San Francisco I told you about," Carter had said. "You come along and swim."

"I don't feel like swimming."

"Maria," Carter had said finally, "he's going to maybe put up some money. Maybe. All right?"

When they walked into the beach house she thought there must have been some misunderstanding, some mixup of time or day, because the man to whom Carter spoke was sitting alone with a projector in the darkened living room running a blue movie of extraordinary technical quality.

"Stroke of two, very prompt," the man had said, and looked at Maria for a long while before he turned off the projector.

"Did you get by the studio yesterday?" Carter seemed oblivious to the meeting's peculiar circumstance. "They show you the rough cut?"

"Fantastic."

"Did Helene see it?" Carter persisted. "Where's Helene?"

"On the beach."

"I'll get my suit on," Maria said, uneasy in the darkened room, and BZ had looked at her again, then flicked the projector back on.

"It's too cold to swim," he said, and then to Carter: "The rough cut looked fantastic, except you're missing the story."

"Meaning what."

"Meaning," BZ said, "how did Maria feel about the gangbang, the twelve cocks, did she get the sense they're doing it not to her but to each *other*, does that *interest* her, you don't get that, you're missing the story."

The reel had run out and the only sound was the film slapping against the projector. "It's a commercial piece, BZ," Carter said finally.

BZ only shrugged, and changed the reel. Again the figures flooded the screen. Wordlessly, BZ sat on a pillow and began watching Maria. He rolled a cigarette and passed it to her, and when she passed it on to Carter he took it without looking away from the screen. Between the marijuana and the figures on the screen Maria felt flushed and not entirely in control.

"Look at the film, BZ," Carter had said suddenly. "Incredible, they've got opticals."

"I've seen the *film*, Carter," BZ had said, and never took his eyes from Maria.

40

"Let's go to Mexico City tonight," BZ said.

"Who?"

"You, me, Helene, I don't know, maybe Larry Kulik, just fly down for a couple of days, Susannah Wood's there now doing some interiors at Churubusco."

"I don't want to do that," Maria said.

"Yes you do," BZ said.

41

EVERY NIGHT she named to herself what she must do: she must ask Les Goodwin to come keep her from peril. Calmed, she would fall asleep pretending that even then she lay with him in a house by the sea. The house was like none she had ever seen but she thought of it so often that she knew even where the linens were kept, the plates, knew how the wild grass ran down to the beach and where the rocks made tidal pools. Every morning in that house she would make the bed with fresh sheets. Every day in that house she would cook while Kate did her lessons. Kate would sit in a shaft of sunlight, her head bent over a pine table, and later when the tide ran out they would gather mussels together, Kate and Maria, and still later all three of them would sit down together at the big pine table and Maria would light a kerosene lamp and they would eat the mussels and drink a bottle of cold white wine and after a while it would be time to lie down again, on the clean white sheets. In the story

Maria told herself at three or four in the morning there were only three people and none of them had histories, only the man and the woman and the child and, in the lamplight, the opalescent mussel shells.

But by dawn she was always back in the house in Beverly Hills, uneasy in the queer early light, plagued by her own and his own and Kate's own manifold histories, certain that BZ and Larry Kulik and all their kind recognized her in a way that Les Goodwin might not want to, recognized her, knew her, had her number, understood as she did that the still center of the daylight world was never a house by the sea but the corner of Sunset and La Brea. In that empty sunlight Kate could do no lessons, and the mussels on any shore Maria knew were toxic. Instead of calling Les Goodwin she bought a silver vinyl dress, and tried to stop thinking about *what had he done with the baby. The tissue. The living dead thing, whatever you called it.*

42

"I'M GOING TO NEW YORK for a few days," she said to Carter. Going to New York had not before occurred to her but in the instant's confusion of running into Carter on the street in Beverly Hills the idea simultaneously materialized and assumed a real plausibility. It was something people did when they did not know what else to do, they went to New York for a few days. "Tomorrow morning," she added.

"What are you going to do in New York?"

"What do people usually do in New York."

He looked at her for a long time. She was aware that her hair was unkempt, her face puffy. She did not meet his eyes.

"They see a few plays," he said finally. "Maybe you can see a few plays."

"Maybe I can," she said, and walked away.

All that day Maria thought of fetuses in the East River, translucent as jellyfish, floating past the big sewage outfalls with the orange peels. She did not go to New York.

43

ONCE A LONG TIME BEFORE Maria had worked a week in Ocho Rios with a girl who had just had an abortion. She could remember the girl telling her about it while they sat huddled next to a waterfall waiting for the photographer to decide the sun was high enough to shoot. It seemed that it was a hard time for abortions in New York, there had been arrests, no one wanted to do it. Finally the girl, her name was Ceci Delano, had asked a friend in the District Attorney's office if he knew of anyone. "Quid pro quo," he had said, and, late the same day that Ceci Delano testified to a blue-ribbon jury that she had been approached by a party-girl operation, she was admitted to Doctors' Hospital for a legal D & C, arranged and paid for by the District Attorney's office.

It had seemed a funny story as she told it, both that morning by the waterfall and later at dinner, when she repeated it to the photographer and the agency man and the fashion coordinator for the client. Maria tried now to put what had happened in Encino into the same spirited perspective, but Ceci Delano's situation seemed not to apply. In the end it was just a New York story.

44

THE LETTER from the hypnotist was mimeographed, and came to Maria in care of the studio that had released *Angel Beach*. "YOUR WORRIES MAY DATE FROM WHEN YOU WERE A BABY," the letter began, and then, after a space, were the words "IN YOUR MOTHER'S WOMB." Maria read the letter very carefully. The hypnotist had found that many people could be regressed not only to infancy but to the very instant of their conception. The hypnotist would receive a few interested clients in the privacy of his Silverlake home. With a sense that she was about to confirm a nightmare, Maria telephoned the number he gave.

45

"You've been brushing it wet," the hairdresser said, lifting a strand of Maria's hair and letting it drop with distaste.

"I guess so." Maria could never keep up her end of the dialogue with hairdressers.

"I told you before, you split the ends," he said with no real interest, and then transferred his attention to a thin girl who had just come up and kissed the back of his neck. "How are you, babe."

"I had an operation."

"No kidding."

"Pelvic abscess." The girl loosened her wrapper and absently stroked her collarbone. "All through my tubes."

"Listen, I hear his new act is just lying there," the hairdresser said. "Bibi Markel was just over there and she heard they were trying to transfer his contract to the lounge."

"*Macht nicht* to me," the girl said. "Except maybe

I'll have to go to court for the separate maintenance." She slipped one big roller away from her scalp and touched the hair to see if it was dry. "Listen," she said suddenly. "Finish her and then comb me out and come up for a drink on your way home."

"Where you living now."

"Off Coldwater, same place. O.K.? Promise?"

"I'll think about it."

"Please. Promise."

He ignored her, and handed Maria a mirror. "You want to use a drier, Maria honey?"

But Maria only shook her head and took the fifteen dollars from her bag and walked very fast toward the dressing room.

"Maybe I can get Sandy to come up." Even from the dressing room Maria could hear the girl wheedling, the thin beautiful girl with the pelvic abscess and the separate maintenance and her hair all done and nobody to drink with. She fixed her attention on the mounds of used wrappers and damp towels and tried not to hear whatever it was the girl would say next. The girl was a presentiment of something. "*Listen,*" the girl said then. "*Maybe I can get Bibi Markel.*"

46

She had watched them in supermarkets and she knew the signs. At seven o'clock on a Saturday evening they would be standing in the checkout line reading the horoscope in *Harper's Bazaar* and in their carts would be a single lamb chop and maybe two cans of cat food and the Sunday morning paper, the early edition with the comics wrapped outside. They would be very pretty some of the time, their skirts the right length and their sunglasses the right tint and maybe only a little vulnerable tightness around the mouth, but there they were, one lamb chop and some cat food and the morning paper. To avoid giving off the signs, Maria shopped always for a household, gallons of grapefruit juice, quarts of green chile salsa, dried lentils and alphabet noodles, rigatoni and canned yams, twenty-pound boxes of laundry detergent. She knew all the indices to the idle lonely, never bought a small tube of toothpaste, never dropped a magazine in her shopping cart. The house in Beverly Hills overflowed with sugar, corn-muffin mix, frozen roasts and Spanish onions. Maria ate cottage cheese.

47

"You're lying in water," the hypnotist said. "You're lying in water and it's warm and you hear your mother's voice."

"No," Maria said. "I don't."

The hypnotist stood up. He always seemed cold and he was always sipping Pernod and water and his house was dusty and cluttered with torn newspaper clippings and stained file folders. "What do you hear," he said finally. "What do you hear and see in your mind right now. What are you doing."

"I'm driving over here," Maria said. "I'm driving Sunset and I'm staying in the left lane because I can see the New Havana Ballroom and I'm going to turn left at the New Havana Ballroom. That's what I'm doing."

48

THERE WAS AT FIRST that spring an occasional faggot who would take her to parties. Never a famous faggot, never one of those committed months in advance to escorting the estranged wives of important directors, but a third-string faggot. At first she was even considered a modest asset by several of them: they liked her not only because she would listen to late-night monologues about how suicidal they felt but because the years she spent modeling had versed her in precisely the marginal distinctions which preoccupied them. She understood, for example, about shoes, and could always distinguish among the right bracelet and the amusing impersonation of the right bracelet and the bracelet that was merely a witless copy. Still, there remained some fatal lack of conviction in her performance, some instant of flushed inattention that would provoke them finally to a defensive condescension. Eventually they would raise their eyebrows helplessly at one another when they were with her, and be oversolicitous. "Darling," they would say, "have another drink." And she would. She was drinking a good deal in the evenings now because when she drank she did not dream. "This way to the gas, ladies and gentlemen," a loudspeaker kept repeating in her dreams now, and she would be checking off names as the children filed past her, the little children in the green antechamber, she would be collecting their lockets and baby rings in a fine mesh basket. Her instructions were to whisper a few comforting words to those children who cried or held back, because this was a humane operation.

49

"LEONARD'S IN NEW YORK for ten days," Helene said as soon as Maria had hung up the telephone. "Did I tell you?"

"Three times," Maria said. Leonard was Helene's hairdresser.

"I don't mind if I'm out of town, but if I'm *in* town and Leonard's *not*—who was that on the telephone?"

"Somebody's leg man."

"What do you mean, somebody's? Whose?"

"Some columnist in the trades. I don't know."

"What did he want?"

"He wanted to know if I was dating anyone in particular. He also wanted to know what I thought of Carter's dating Susannah Wood."

Helene shrugged. "You knew that."

"I mean the word *dating*? Doesn't it strike you funny?"

"Not particularly." Helene was studying her hair

line in a small mirror. "If I'm *in* town, and Leonard's *not*, I feel almost . . . frightened."

Maria said nothing.

"I don't suppose you understand that."

Maria watched the tears welling in Helene's eyes. "Don't, Helene," she said finally. "Don't be depressed."

"It's shit," Helene said. "It's all shit."

50

EVERYTHING MARIA could think to do in the town she had already done. She had checked into the motel, she had eaten a crab at the marina. At three in the afternoon she had been the only customer in the marina restaurant and it had been a dispiriting thirty or forty minutes, sliced beets staining the crab legs and a couple of waitresses arguing listlessly and a piped medley from *Showboat*. After that she had walked on the gravelly sand and she had driven aimlessly to Port Hueneme and back to Oxnard and now she sat on a bench in the downtown plaza, watching some boys in ragged Levi jackets and dark goggles who sat on the grass near her car. Their Harleys were pulled up to the curb and they seemed to be passing a joint with furtive daring and every now and then they would look over at her and laugh. Because there was an oil fire somewhere to the north a yellow haze hung over the town, a stillness over the plaza. On the next bench an old man coughed soundlessly, spit phlegm that seemed to hang in the heavy air. A woman in a nurse's uniform wheeled a bundled neuter figure silently past the hedges of dead camellias. Maria closed her eyes and imagined the woman coming toward her with a hypodermic needle. When she opened her eyes again the boys in the Levi jackets seemed to be rifling the glove compartments of parked cars. To hear the sound of her own footsteps Maria stood up and walked to the pay phone by the public toilet and asked the operator to try the number in Los Angeles again.

She would tell him she could not wait.

She would tell him she was sitting in a park watching some hoods rifling cars and she could not wait.

Maybe she would not feel this way if she talked to him, maybe he would make her laugh. Maybe she would hear his voice and the silence would break, the woman in the nurse's uniform would speak to her charge and the boys would get on their Harleys and roar off.

But when the operator got the studio a voice said only that Mr. Goodwin could not be reached.

When she hung up the phone the silence was absolute. The boys in the Levi jackets were all watching her now, because they were standing around her car, they knew it was her car, they had watched her lock it. They were trying various keys. They were watching to see what she would do. As if in slowed motion she began walking across the grass toward the car, and as she got closer they melted back, formed a semicircle. Abstractly she admired the way that she and they together were evolving a choreography, hearing the same silent beat. She kept her eyes steady, her pace even, and when she found herself unlocking the car under their blank gaze it was with extreme deliberation. As she slid into the driver's seat she stared directly at each of them, one by one, and in that instant of total complicity one of them leaned across the hood and raised a hand in recognition of what had passed between them, his palm out, inscribing an arc in the still air. Later those few minutes in the plaza in Oxnard would come back to Maria and she would replay them, change the scenario. It ended that way badly, or well, depending on what you wanted.

51

SHE SAT IN THE MOTEL ROOM near the Southern Pacific tracks in Oxnard and waited for Les Goodwin to call. He had said nine-thirty or ten but she had driven past the theater in the afternoon, the marquee read MAJOR STUDIO PREVIEW 8 p.m. An eight o'clock sneak meant eleven, by the time they counted the cards. When the telephone rang, it was quarter to eleven and he said it would be another half hour. Maria took two Librium, washed her face although she had showered an hour before, straightened the immaculate room as if to erase any sign of herself. When there was nothing left to straighten she walked across the parking lot to the ice machine by the swimming pool and filled a paper bucket with ice. After she had arranged the bucket on a tray with two water glasses and a bottle of whisky she sat on the bed and turned the pages of the Oxnard–Port Hueneme telephone book. There were fourteen Wyeths listed, twenty-three Langs and twenty Goodwins.

When she finally opened the door for him she avoided his eyes, buried her face against his shirt. They were both shaking. He poured Scotch into the two glasses without ice and they sat down on the bed and still they had not looked at each other.

"I almost didn't come," he said then. "I called the house this afternoon, I was going to tell you I wasn't coming up, they'd canceled the preview."

"I know."

"You know."

"I was going to tell you I was here and couldn't wait."

"You came up this afternoon?"

"I didn't have anything in particular to do in town," she said, and then she looked at him. "I came up this afternoon because I was afraid you'd call me up and tell me they'd canceled the preview."

"This is a lousy place," he said finally. "Let's get out of here."

They drove up the coast until they were exhausted enough to sleep, and then they did sleep, wrapped together like children in a room by the sea in Morro Bay.

"I've got until tomorrow, we can go on up the coast," he said the next morning.

"We could go up to Big Sur."

"We could have a picnic, we could stay at the Lodge."

"We could buy a sleeping bag and sleep on the beach."

"I've got to call Felicia," he said then.

"Wait until I'm dressed."

She dressed with her back to him, then left the motel room and walked down to the water. A culvert had washed out and the equipment brought in to lift it was mired in the sandy mud. Bare-legged and bare-armed, shivering in her cotton jersey dress, she stood for a long while watching them try to free the equipment. When she got back to the motel he was dressed, sitting on the unmade bed.

"Don't cry," he said.

"There's no point."

"No point in what."

"No point in our doing any of those things."

He looked at her for a long while. "Later," he said then.

"I'm sorry."

"It's all right."

On the drive back they told each other that it had been the wrong time, the wrong place, that it was bad because he had lied to arrange it, that it would be all right another time, idyllic later. He mentioned the strain he had been under, he mentioned that the preview had gone badly. She mentioned that she was getting the curse. They mentioned Kate, Carter, Felicia, the weather, Oxnard, his dislike of motel rooms, her fear of subterfuge. They mentioned everything but one thing: that she had left the point in a bedroom in Encino.

52

MARIA MADE A LIST of things she would never do. She would never: *walk through the Sands or Caesar's alone after midnight.* She would never: *ball at a party, do S-M unless she wanted to, borrow furs from Abe Lipsey, deal.* She would never: *carry a Yorkshire in Beverly Hills.*

53

"I'LL BE AWAY a few weeks," Carter said. "I came by because I'll be away, I wanted to tell you—you know the picture's entered at Cannes."

"I read that."

"You seen it yet?"

"How would I have seen it, it's not in release, I mean is it?"

"Maria, for Christ's fucking sake, they've been screening it every night for a month, you know that—oh shit."

"I didn't mean to be that way," she said after a while.

"You never mean to be any way."

It was always that way when he came by but sometimes later, after he had left, the spectre of his joyless face would reach her, talk about heart's needle, would flash across her hapless consciousness all the images of the family they might have been: Carter throwing a clear plastic ball filled with confetti, Kate missing the ball. Kate crying. Carter swinging Kate by her wrists. The spray from the sprinklers and the clear plastic ball with the confetti falling inside and Kate's fat arms stretched up again for the catch she would always miss. Freeze frame. Kate fevered, Carter sponging her back while Maria called the pediatrician. Kate's birthday, Kate laughing, Carter blowing out the candle. The images would flash at Maria like slides in a dark room. On film they might have seemed a family.

"Listen," Maria said to Carter the night before he left for Cannes. She had put off calling until almost midnight but had finally made herself do it. "The picture's fine. I went to a screening, it's a beautiful picture."

There was a silence. "If you need to reach me call BZ," he said then. "He'll know where I am."

"The picture. I really liked it."

"Fine. Thanks."

"What's the matter."

"Just forget it, Maria." His voice was tired. "There hasn't been a print in Los Angeles all week."

During the next few weeks Maria bought *Daily Variety* and *The Hollywood Reporter* and studied them dutifully for small mentions of Carter. After Cannes he seemed to be in London, and after that in Paris again, where he appeared on television discussing the *auteur* principle.

"Carter's staying another week in Paris, I guess you know," Helene said on the telephone.

"The touring *auteur*," Maria said.

Helene paused only slightly. "BZ called them last night, apparently she has to stay over to talk about a picture."

"I suppose he was pleased about Cannes."

"He didn't talk about it much but she said—"

"You think you're telling me something, Helene, you're missing the point."

Helene giggled. "Whose point."

That afternoon Maria had a small accident with the Corvette, received a call from the bank about her overdrawn account, and learned from the drugstore that the doctor would no longer renew her barbiturate prescriptions. In a way she was relieved.

54

Maria stood in the sun on the Western street and waited for the young agent from Freddy Chaikin's office to back his Volkswagen past the Writers' Building to where she was. It was hot and no one had left her name at the gate and there was a spot on her skirt and she was annoyed because of the trouble at the gate and because Freddy Chaikin had not come himself. He had arranged for her to see a director who wanted her for a bike picture and the least he could have done was show up himself. She did not even want to do another bike picture.

"Looks like we missed him," the young agent said. He did not turn the motor off.

"How do you mean, we missed him."

"I mean I guess he's already left for lunch." The agent looked uncomfortably past Maria. "Actually it wasn't two hundred percent confirmed, he told Freddy he might be tied up with the girl they're looking at for the lead."

Maria pushed her hair back and watched the agent avoid her eyes. "What exactly did they want me for," she said finally.

"The high-school teacher, Freddy must've told you that. You read the script, that's the *part,* the lead's just any teeny fluff. I mean the *teacher,* she . . . she carries the picture."

"The teacher," Maria said. "Who plays the Angel Mama?"

"His girlfriend."

"I have to go now," Maria said, and without waiting for him to speak she turned and began walking toward the gate. Once in her car she drove as far as Romaine and then pulled over, put her head on the steering wheel and cried as she had not cried since she was a child, cried out loud. She cried because she was humiliated and she cried for her mother and she cried for Kate and she cried because something had just come through to her, there in the sun on the Western street: she had deliberately not counted the months but she must have been counting them unawares, must have been keeping a relentless count somewhere, because this was the day, the day the baby would have been born.

55

"I WANT TO TELL YOU right now I'm never going to do anything again," Ivan Costello had said in the beginning. "If you want to live that way, O.K. There's not going to be any money and there's not going to be any eating breakfast together and there's not going to be any getting married and there's not going to be any baby makes three. And if you make any money, I'll spend it."

She had said she wanted to live that way.

"What if I did," she had said a long time later.

"Did what."

"Got pregnant. Then at least I'd have a baby."

"No you wouldn't," he had said.

56

"Maybe next time," the hypnotist said. "Next week."

"I'm not coming next week." Maria did not look at him. "I can't come any more."

The hypnotist watched her as she opened her bag, found her car keys, dropped them beneath a sofa cushion and groped for them. The room was overheated but he was wearing two faded cardigan sweaters and standing over a furnace vent.

"It doesn't prove anything, you know," he said.

"What doesn't."

"That you couldn't open enough doors to get back. Your failure. It doesn't prove anything at all."

"I have to leave."

He shrugged. As she stood up he was pouring water into a cheese glass coated with Pernod, swirling the mixture into a milky fluid.

"Some people resist," he said. "Some people don't want to know."

Maria drove down to the New Havana Ballroom on Sunset and, trembling, made a telephone call.

"I need help," she said. "Ivan, I need help bad."

57

"WHO'S YOUR FRIEND," Ivan Costello said. "Who loves you."

It was five o'clock in Los Angeles and eight in New York and he was drunk. She should have known better than to call him. She did not even like him. She could not bring herself to give the answer he expected, could not pick up the old litany, could not say *you do*.

"I don't know," she said.

"What's the matter with you."

"I just wanted to talk to you."

"You just wanted . . ." He paused, and she knew that he was turning on her. "To *talk* to me."

She said nothing. The bar in the New Havana was empty and smelled of disinfectant and the bartender was watching her distrustfully.

"You mean you want to talk to me direct, you don't want me to make an appointment? Go through your agent?"

"All right. I get it."

"You're *feeling* good enough to talk to me? You aren't sick? You aren't asleep? You aren't out of town? You aren't just fucking una*vai*lable?"

"Ivan—"

" 'Ivan' *shit.*"

"All right," she said. "O.K."

"You want to know what I think of your life?"

"No," she said, but he was already spitting into the telephone.

In the morning he left four messages on the service and Maria returned none of them. She did call Larry Kulik.

58

MARIA SAT ON A COUCH in the ladies' room of the Flamingo with the attendant and a Cuban who was killing the hour between her ten o'clock and midnight dates and she knew that she could not go back out to the crap tables.

"Like a cemetery," the Cuban said.

The attendant shrugged. "Every place the same."

"Not the Sands, I could hardly get through the Sands tonight."

"So do business at the Sands."

"Fucking negrita," the Cuban said without rancor, and looked at Maria appraisingly. "You sick? You need something?"

"I'm all right," Maria said. "Thank you."

She could not go back to the tables because Benny Austin was out there. Somehow she had never expected to see Benny Austin again: in her mind he was always in her father's pickup, or standing with her mother and father on the tarmac at McCarran waving at the wrong window. There was something wrong with running into Benny Austin in the Flamingo. "Maria?" he had called when he saw her. "*Maria?* That you?" He was shorter than she remembered him, shorter and more frail, almost bald, a failed man wearing a lariat tie clasp. "Jesus if you aren't the picture of Francine," he kept saying. "Jesus but you're her daughter." He had asked her if she was married. He had shrugged and said that the course of true love never was a straight flush. He had ordered Cuba Libres for the two of them and he had talked about *as it was* and finally she had run. He would be waiting there still, trying to run up a stake for her with the chips she had left, that was like Benny, he would play her chips until they were gone and then he would play his own for her, waiting, holding the Cuba Libre until the ice was gone. Benny would wait there all night. Benny would lay anybody in the Flamingo five-to-one that Harry and Francine Wyeth's daughter would not run out on him, and five-to-one were the best odds Benny would lay on the sun rising.

When Maria heard herself being paged she asked the Cuban for a match and gave no sign that she was Maria Wyeth. Maybe it was Benny paging her but having people paged was not much Benny's style, more likely it was Larry Kulik. She smoked a cigarette and tried not to think about Benny hearing her name and looking around, adjusting his tie clasp and holding his bets, wondering who was calling Harry and Francine's girl, waiting for her to reappear and introduce her friend, make it an evening. After Maria had finished the cigarette she took a back elevator up to Larry Kulik's suite.

59

"TELL HIM TO COME UP," Larry Kulik said, handing her a drink while she waited for the operator to page Benny Austin. In the other room there were some of Larry Kulik's well-manicured friends and a couple of girls, one of them the Cuban she had seen in the ladies' room. The Cuban had given her no sign of recognition. "Guys like that interest me, you'd be surprised."

"I wouldn't be surprised at all. Tell that spic to turn the music down."

She waited. "Benny?" She raised her voice over the clatter of the slot machines downstairs. "Benny, I got sick, I—"

"Christ, Maria, why didn't you say something, I got a good friend, house doctor at the Mint."

"I just need some rest. Benny? Can you hear me? You come see me the next time you're in Los Angeles, all right? Promise?"

"Sure, honey, swell. I'd like that."

Maria felt a rush of shame. Benny Austin never

came to Los Angeles. "Listen," she said suddenly. "You remember the last time you saw me? Remember? You and Mother and Daddy put me on the plane at McCarran? And before that we ate spare ribs at the house? Remember?"

"Sure, honey, you bet. Next time I'm over we'll paint the town."

For a long while Maria lay on the bed and stared at a large oil painting of a harlequin. In a sense the day they ate spare ribs and drove to McCarran had ceased to exist, had never happened at all: she was the only one left who remembered it. Maria followed this thought for as far as it would go, which was not very far, and then she got up and opened the door. A second-string comedian had come in with some of his entourage, and a girl Maria had seen drinking in the lounge.

"New talent," the comedian said, looking at Maria.

"She's not talent," Larry Kulik said.

At dawn she woke Larry Kulik and told him she was taking the seven o'clock flight out.

"Stick around," he said. "What is it with you, you want to get paid for your time or something? So I crapped out on you last night. So what."

"That's not it."

"Suit yourself," Larry Kulik said.

60

At a party in May she left not with the choreo-
grapher who had brought her but with an actor she
had never before met. They had danced together and
shared a joint in the garden and he told her that they
would leave and go up to his house. He had some
friends there. Maria was wearing the silver vinyl dress
she had bought to make her feel better and her hair
was loose and her feet were bare and driving up
through the canyon in the actor's Ferrari she felt good
for the first time in a long while. The actor had a
tape in the car that played *Midnight Hour* over and
over again and when they got to his house he introduced her to the eight or ten people in the living
room as Myra. "This is Myra," he said. "I just found
her some place." Four or five joints were being passed
in the living room and she smoked one and then went
to find a Coca-Cola. In the kitchen she danced by
herself and felt a little dizzy but still good. She liked

his not knowing her. She did not much like him but she liked his not knowing her.

"Let's fuck," the actor said from the doorway.

"You mean right here."

"Not here, in the bed." He seemed annoyed.

She shook her head.

"Then do it here," he said. "Do it with the Coke bottle."

When they finally did it they were on the bed and at the moment before he came he reached under the pillow and pulled out an amyl nitrite popper and broke it under his nose, breathed in rapidly, and closed his eyes.

"Don't move," he said. "*I said don't move.*"

Maria did not move.

"Terrific," he said then. His eyes were still closed.

Maria said nothing.

"Wake me up in three hours," he said. "With your tongue."

After he had gone to sleep she got dressed very quietly and walked out of the house. She was in the driveway before she remembered that she had no car. The keys were in his Ferrari and she took it, hesitating when she came out to the main canyon road, turning then not toward Beverly Hills but toward the Valley, and the freeway. It was dawn before she reached Vegas and, because she stopped in Vegas to buy cigarettes, eight o'clock before she reached Tonopah. She was not sure what she had meant to do in Tonopah. There was something about seeing her mother's and father's graves, but her mother and father were not buried in Tonopah. They were buried in Silver Wells, or what had been Silver Wells. In any case she was stopped for speeding outside Tonopah and when the highway patrolman saw the silver dress and the bare feet and the Ferrari registered to someone else, he checked California to see if the car had been reported stolen, and it had.

61

THEY LET HER make one call, and she called Freddy
Chaikin. It was not as easy for Freddy to fix as it
might have been, because when they vacuumed the
car they picked up marijuana, but still, by sundown,
she was flying back across the desert with Freddy in a
Lear he had borrowed from a client. Freddy had done
everything. Freddy had driven out to the Malibu ranch
where the actor was shooting a Western and had told
the actor whom to call to retract the complaint. Freddy had waited there while the actor did it. Freddy
had gotten in touch with one of the big savings-and-
loan Democrats, who got in touch with someone in
Nevada and the marijuana came off the report. And
now as the jet gained altitude Freddy was handing
Maria a drink. She was still wearing the silver dress
and she was still barefoot and her face was streaked
with dust and when she tasted the drink it all came
up, all the pills and the not eating and the liquor and
the fear and the way she had felt about the actor and

the way she had felt when the matron had her finger up her looking for drugs, all that came up in a trail of mucous on the floor of the Lear that Freddy had borrowed in his day-long effort to protect Carter. Freddy watched her clean it up.

"I don't understand girls like you," he said finally.

She clutched a towel to her mouth but the convulsion passed.

"I mean there's something in your behavior, Maria, I would almost go so far as to call it . . ." Freddy paused, and lit a cigarillo with his gold Cartier lighter. When he spoke again he measured each word. "Almost go so far as to call it a very self-destructive personality structure."

Maria closed her eyes. "You know what, Freddy?"

"What."

"I'd almost go so far as to call you—"

Freddy Chaikin flicked the gold lighter closed and smiled at her.

Maria took his hand, and went to sleep.

62

Two dozen roses arrived from the actor, or rather from his business manager. Maria knew that the business manager had sent them because his name was on the delivery slip.

"Hey, babe," the actor said when he called. "You didn't have to call out the tactical nukes."

"I don't know what you're talking about."

"I'm talking about Freddy Chaikin, he shows up at ten o'clock in the morning and tries to lay it on me I'll never be in a package with any of his clients again. I mean I was *shoot*ing."

"I was in *jail.*"

"Just hold on, cunt," the actor said, his voice rising. "*You never told me who you were.*"

"I hear you had a rather baroque morning-after," Helene said.

Helene came to the house all the time now. Sometimes Maria would pretend no one was home but today Helene had walked in without ringing and come directly upstairs. She sat on the edge of the bed and took out a cigarette.

"How exactly did you hear that," Maria said finally. She had taken so many showers during the past several hours that her skin felt damp between the sheets, but the smell of Helene's cigarette and perfume was making her feel dirty again. "I mean what exactly did you hear."

"Just that. Carter called from New York and told BZ."

"I haven't even talked to Carter."

"Freddy did, naturally." Helene picked up Maria's lipstick and studied the effect of the color on the back of her wrist. "I mean Freddy is seriously worried about you, Carter is seriously worried about you, BZ and *I* are—"

"I'm *all right*."

"Of course. You're really on top of it. I mean for example there's nothing at all peculiar about hiding here under the covers shaking at three o'clock in the afternoon. Nothing at all off about leaving a party with Johnny Waters and ending up in jail in Nevada at eight o'clock the next morning. Nothing wrong there."

"I've got a headache. I'm in bed because my head aches."

"I'll get a Darvon."

Maria pulled the sheet up to her chin.

"I'm just trying to help you, Maria."

"I'll be all right." Maria sat up and touched Helene's arm. "Really, Helene. I promise."

"All right, never mind, I'm leaving." Helene stood up and smoothed the bed where she had been sitting and then stared at herself for a long while in the mirror on the dressing-room door. "What kind of fuck is Johnny Waters?" she asked finally.

During the next week Freddy Chaikin made a number of telephone calls to various television producers asking, "as a personal favor to Carter," that Maria be considered for parts, even day work. "Anything to take her mind off herself," Freddy said to each of them. "What we've got here is a slightly suicidal situation." Maria knew about these calls because Helene told her about them.

"I saw a picture of you today," Helene said.

"Where." Every time she went downstairs Helene seemed to be there.

"You know that employment agency on Beverly? The one where you got the Guatemalan who stole your diaphragm?"

"I don't know." Maria did not want to think about the Guatemalan who had taken her diaphragm.

"You do too know. They've got all those studio stills on the wall? Satisfied customers? Anyway, now they've got a picture of you, signed 'Good luck, Maria Wyeth.' "

"Well, fine," Maria said. "I didn't think you'd be in town again today."

Helene looked at her and giggled. "BZ sent me," she said finally. "BZ wants me to get you to spend a few weeks at the beach."

Maria said nothing.

"You looked years younger in this picture, I must say." Helene laughed again. " 'Good luck, Maria Wyeth.' "

"*Dear Maria,*" the note read. "*Well don't know when I'll get over to LA but wanted to give you a telephone where you can call if you are in Nevada again or need help. Have some things of your Dad's I want to give you, also because you are like my own daughter there will be a little windfall from this quarter some day, not too soon let's hope. Have all your Dad's papers plus mineral certificates, no action now but quien sabe, once knew a man who thought his rights were worthless and he was sitting on pitchblende so loaded with U. the counters went haywire.*

Call me at number below and ask for Benny, phone belongs to lady next door, also she cooks for me sometimes. Not like your Mom. Ha ha. Your Friend Benny C. Austin."

Maria was listening to someone talk and every now and then she would hear herself making what she thought was an appropriate response but mostly she was just swaying slightly with the music and wondering where her drink was when suddenly Felicia Goodwin took her arm.

"We're leaving now, Maria. We'll drop you."

"I have my car, thanks, I'm fine."

"Les?" Felicia was talking over her shoulder. "I need you."

Maria picked up someone else's drink and smiled past Felicia at Les. "Crowd scene," she said. "Principals emerge."

"You come with Felicia and me, Maria. I'll get your car tomorrow."

Maria put the glass down and looked at him for a long while.

"I didn't come with you," she said very clearly then. "Thank Christ."

After that she was crying, and Helene was holding her arm while BZ got her coat.

"I thought it merited a mention," Felicia Goodwin whispered.

"Let it *go*," Helene said. Grateful, Maria put her head on Helene's shoulder and let herself be led outside. In the car she was sick on Helene's lap, and told BZ he was a degenerate.

When she woke before dawn in Helene's bedroom she saw that someone had undressed and bathed and creamed her body. At first she thought she was alone in the room but then she saw BZ and Helene, sprawled together on a chaise. She had only the faintest ugly memory of what had brought BZ and Helene together, and to erase it from her mind she fixed her imagination on a needle dripping sodium pentathol into her arm and began counting backward from one hundred. When that failed she imagined herself driving, conceived audacious lane changes, strategic shifts of gear, the Hollywood to the San Bernardino and straight on out, past Barstow, past Baker, driving straight on into the hard white empty core of the world. She slept and did not dream.

63

"I GUESS I DRANK too much last night," Maria said carefully.

"Don't talk about it." Helene was staring out the kitchen window, holding a cup of coffee in her two hands as if for warmth. Her eyes were puffy and there was a bruise on her left cheekbone and her voice was soft and vague. "I don't want to talk about it. The wind makes me feel bad."

"I just don't remember getting here." Maria had a flash image of BZ holding a belt and Helene laughing and she tried not to look at the bruise on Helene's face. "That's all I was saying."

Tears began falling down Helene's face. "Don't *talk* about it. And don't say you don't remember, either."

"I didn't—" Maria broke off. BZ was standing in the doorway.

"I picked up your car." BZ dropped the keys on the table and looked from Maria to Helene. "What have we here," he said softly. "A little hangover terror? A few second thoughts? Is that about the size of it?"

Helene said nothing.

"I can't take this, Helene." BZ was wearing tinted glasses and for the first time Maria noticed a sag beneath his eyes. "If you can't deal with the morning, get out of the game. You've been around a long time, you know what it is, it's play-or-pay."

"Why don't you go tell that to Carlotta," Helene whispered.

Maria closed her eyes at the instant BZ's hand hit Helene's face. "Stop it," she screamed.

BZ looked at Maria and laughed. "You weren't talking that way last night," he said.

64

F ROM A PAY PHONE on the highway outside Las Vegas she called the number Benny Austin had given her. The number was no longer in service.

"You here all alone?" the bellboy in the Sands asked, lingering after she had tipped him.

"My husband's meeting me here."

"Is that right? Today? Tomorrow?"

She looked at him. "Go away," she said.

The room was painted purple, with purple Lurex threads in the curtains and bedspread. Because her mother had once told her that purple rooms could send people into irreversible insanity she thought about asking for a different room, but the boy had unnerved her. She did not want to court further appraisal by asking anyone for anything. To hear someone's voice she looked in the telephone book and dialed a few prayers, then took three aspirin and tried not to think about BZ and Helene.

In the morning she went to the post office. Because it was Saturday the long corridors were deserted, and all but one of the grilled windows shuttered. Her sandals clattered against the marble and echoed as she walked.

"Could you put this in Box 674," she said to the clerk at the one open window. 674 was the number on the envelope of Benny Austin's letter.

"Can't."

"Why not."

"It's got to have postage. It's got to go through the United States mail."

Sullenly he studied the nickel and penny she gave him, then pushed one stamp under the grill and watched her stamp the note.

"Now could you put it in 674?"

"No," he said, and threw the letter into a canvas bin.

She found a bench near Box 674 and sat down. At noon the last window slammed shut. Maria drank from the water cooler, smoked cigarettes, read the F.B.I. posters. Wandering the country somewhere were Negro Females Armed with Lye, Caucasian Males posing as Baby Furniture Representatives, Radio Station Employees traveling out of Texas with wives and children and embezzled cash and Schemes for Getting Money and Never Delivering on Piece-work, an inchoate army on the move. Maria crossed the street to a diner with a view of the post office and tried to eat a grilled-cheese sandwich.

On the third day a woman unlocked Box 674. She was wearing a soiled white uniform and she had a hard sad face and Maria did not want to speak to her.

"Excuse me," she said finally. "I'm trying to reach Benny Austin—"

"What *is* this." The woman was holding Maria's letter and her eyes darted from the letter to Maria.

"Actually I sent that letter—"

"And now you want it back."

"No. Not at all. I want you to give it to Benny Austin and tell—"

"I don't know any Benny person. And I think it's pretty funny this letter addressed to some Benny person in my box and then right off you sashay up and start dropping the same name, either you've been tampering in my box, a federal offense, or you're trying some other mickey mouse and believe me you've got the wrong party."

Maria backed away. The woman's face was white and twisted and she was following Maria, her voice rising. "You're Luanne's foster mother, is exactly who you are, and you're nosing around Vegas because you heard about the injury settlement, well just you *forget it*. I said *forget it*."

65

"WHAT DO YOU THINK," Maria could hear one of the men saying. She was trying to eat an egg roll in the Sands and the two men and the girl had been watching her ever since she sat down.

"About what," the girl said.

"That."

The girl shrugged. "Maybe."

The other man said something that Maria did not hear and when she looked up again the girl was still watching her.

"Thirty-six," the girl said. "But a good thirty-six."

For the rest of the time Maria was in Las Vegas she wore dark glasses. She did not decide to stay in Vegas: she only failed to leave. She spoke to no one. She did not gamble. She neither swam nor lay in the sun. She was there on some business but she could not seem to put her finger on what that business was. All day, most of every night, she walked and she drove. Two or three times a day she walked in and out of all the hotels on the Strip and several downtown. She began to crave the physical flash of walking in and out of places, the temperature shock, the hot wind blowing outside, the heavy frigid air inside. She thought about nothing. Her mind was a blank tape, imprinted daily with snatches of things overheard, fragments of dealers' patter, the beginnings of jokes and odd lines of song lyrics. When she finally lay down nights in the purple room she would play back the day's tape, a girl singing into a microphone and a fat man dropping a glass, cards fanned on a table and a dealer's rake in closeup and a woman in slacks crying and the opaque blue eyes of the guard at some baccarat table. A child in the harsh light of a crosswalk on the Strip. A sign on Fremont Street. A light blinking. In her half sleep the point was ten, the jackpot was on eighteen, *the only man that could ever reach her was the son of a preacher man,* someone was down sixty, someone was up, Daddy wants a popper and she *rode a painted pony let the spinning wheel spin.*

By the end of a week she was thinking constantly about where her body stopped and the air began, about the exact point in space and time that was the difference between *Maria* and *other.* She had the sense that if she could get that in her mind and hold it for even one micro-second she would have what she had come to get. As if she had fever, her skin burned and crackled with a pinpoint sensitivity. She could feel smoke against her skin. She could feel voice waves. She was beginning to feel color, light intensities, and she imagined that she could be put blindfolded in front of the signs at the Thunderbird and the Flamingo and know which was which. "Maria," she felt someone whisper one night, but when she turned there was nobody.

She began to feel the pressure of Hoover Dam, there on the desert, began to feel the pressure and pull of the water. When the pressure got great enough she drove out there. All that day she felt the power surging through her own body. All day she was faint with vertigo, sunk in a world where great power grids converged, throbbing lines plunged finally into the shallow canyon below the dam's face, elevators like coffins dropped into the bowels of the earth itself. With a guide and a handful of children Maria walked through the chambers, stared at the turbines in the vast glittering gallery, at the deep still water with the hidden intakes sucking all the while, even as she watched; clung to the railings, leaned out, stood finally on a platform over the pipe that carried the river beneath the dam. The platform quivered. Her ears roared. She wanted to stay in the dam, lie on the great pipe itself, but reticence saved her from asking.

"Just how long have you been here now," Freddy Chaikin asked when she ran into him in Caesar's. "You planning on making a year of it? Or what?"

"Two weeks, Freddy. I haven't been here *even* two weeks."

"Jesus Christ, two weeks in Vegas."

"I like the good talk."

"I'm over for Lenny's opening, you coming?"

She tried to think who Lenny was. "I'm not seeing too many people, actually."

"That's not healthy, you're morbid enough. Do me a favor, come on over after. Lenny's suite. A *lot* of people you know."

"I'll see."

"Maria. A personal favor. You owe me one, O.K.? 1202, that's in the *new* building."

"Could you tell me how to find 1202," she asked the man at the desk in the hotel. When she had called up from the lobby there was too much noise to understand Freddy's directions.

She waited. The desk clerk did not look up.

"I'm looking for 1202."

He lifted his eyes only slightly. "No," he said.

"You don't understand. I don't know how to get to the new building."

"I do understand, honey. I understand *very well*. No dice. If they want you up there they'd tell you how to get there. Freelance some place else."

When she got back to the Sands she looked at herself in the mirror for a long while, then called room service and asked for a double bourbon. When the boy came he looked at her.

"Pretty early still," he said.

She poured a few drops of bourbon over the ice and watched it coat the glass. It seemed to her now that she had been driving all week toward precisely this instant. "I don't know anyone," she heard herself saying.

"Lots of guys around."

"I don't know any."

"I could make an introduction."

She looked at him. "All right," she said. "In an hour."

After he left she waited five minutes and then walked into the corridor and out onto the burning floodlit parking lot and an hour later she was deep into the desert, driving west at eighty miles an hour. Early in the morning she called Freddy Chaikin from

Los Angeles and asked him to pay her bill and bring back her clothes.

"What happened."

Maria did not answer.

"I don't even want to know," Freddy Chaikin said.

"Don't forget my dark glasses," Maria said.

66

"WHAT DO YOU WEIGH NOW? About eighty-two?"

Maria opened her eyes. The voice was Carter's but for an instant in the bright afternoon light on the sun deck she could not make out his features.

"I didn't know you'd be here today," she said finally.

"Helene told me you were coming out."

"Helene is a veritable Celebrity Register."

"Just calm down. I want to talk about something." He looked back toward the house. BZ was on the telephone in the living room. "Let's walk down the beach."

"We can talk here."

"Have it your way, we can talk here." He kicked aside her sandals and sat down. "I've been trying to get hold of you for two weeks."

"I know it."

"No games, Maria, O.K.? I came all the way out here, I walked out of a meeting, a meeting with Carl Kastner, just to—"

She reached for his hand and put it over his mouth. She was absurdly touched by the detail about Carl Kastner: Carter was still Carter. "I haven't wanted to see you because I didn't feel good. That's all. Talk to me."

Carter took out a cigarette, crumpled the package, then smoothed out the package and replaced the cigarette. "You know I'm starting the new picture on the desert in ten days," he said finally. "You knew about that." He was not looking at her. "Which means this: it means—"

"It means," she prompted after a pause.

He looked at her. "I want you out there."

Maria said nothing.

"We could do it."

"Why should we."

Carter looked uncomfortable. "It just might be better."

"You mean you don't think I can take care of myself."

"No." Carter stood up. "I do not. I do not think you can take care of yourself. Things I've been hearing, things I—"

"What things."

"You know goddamn fucking well what things."

He stood over Maria with his hand frozen in air. He had been about to hit her.

175

"Go ahead," she said. "You can't hurt me."

"Fantastic day," a clear voice said, and Carter dropped his arm. A girl with long tangled hair and a short chemise nightgown stood in the doorway, yawning and shaking out her hair. "You suppose there's any coffee?" The girl examined what seemed to be a bite on her arm and walked out into the sun. "I mean I could die for some."

"I don't know," Maria said.

"BZ honey?" the girl called. "Is there coffee made?"

"No," BZ said from the house. "There is no coffee. There is *not any coffee.*"

"Honey, there must be instant," the girl drawled. From the doorway she smiled back at Carter. "I'm Jeanelle," she said.

"Who the fuck was that," Carter said after a moment.

Maria sat huddled in a towel. "I guess that's Jeanelle."

"Who's she for?"

"*How should I know.*"

Carter looked at her. "Stop it," he said finally. "Stop crying. Baby, listen. Stop."

"I don't know what to do."

"You're going to come to the desert with me."

"Just as a point of interest, you going to be fucking Susannah Wood out there?"

Carter pulled her to her feet and kissed her. She stood without moving and after a while he let his arms drop.

"What's the matter now," he said.

"Nothing."

"It's all gone with you," he said. "It used to be there but it's gone."

"Listen," she said as if by rote. "I love you."

"You know what I wish it was tonight?" the girl in the nightgown was saying when Maria came inside at four o'clock. "I wish it was New Year's Eve. Most people think New Year's Eve is a bore but I love it."

Helene lay on a couch staring at the ceiling. "You do," she said.

"Helene," BZ said. "Maria's going to the desert with us, isn't that interesting?" BZ smiled at Maria. "I said Maria's going to the desert, Helene."

"I heard you."

"I also love Christmas," the girl said.

"Jeanelle," BZ said, "there's some coke in the bedroom if you want to go get it. Some Merck."

"You've been holding out," Jeanelle said.

BZ watched the girl leave and then turned to Helene. "Get her out of here," he said.

Helene stared at him. "You started it," she whispered.

67

"YOU TOLD ME YOU'D COME," Carter said.

"What for."

"I want you out there."

"It's all gone, you said so yourself."

"All right," Carter said. "Stay here and kill yourself.
Something interesting like that."

Carter and BZ and Helene left for the desert.
Maria found a doctor who would give her barbiturates
again, and in the evenings she drove.

"Who is it," she whispered when she saw the lighted
cigar in the dark living room. She had just let herself
into the house and locked the door behind her and
now she leaned against it. "I said who is it."

The cigar moved. She closed her eyes.

"Who do you think it is," Ivan Costello said. "Maybe
if you'd call your answering service once in a while
you'd know when I was in town."

"What are you doing in my house."

"Come here."

She turned on a light.

"I said come here."

"No." She could see that he was drunk. "I'm going out."

"You aren't going anywhere. Don't tell me no."

"No."

"All right," he said. "Fight me. You'll like it better that way anyway."

"What did you come here for," she said at three or four in the morning.

"What I got."

"What did you come here for," she repeated.

"I didn't come here to hurt you, if that's what you mean."

She said nothing.

"Oh Christ," he said. "Baby. I just came to make you remember."

"I can't remember."

"You remembered all right the last three hours."

She wrapped her arms around her bare shoulders. "That hasn't got anything to do with me."

"Baby, it used to."

"Get out of here," she said, and this time he did.

In the morning he came again. She answered the

door and went back to the couch where she had spent the rest of the night.

"You don't have to crack up over this," he said. "You used to tell me you'd do it for me until you died. You used to tell me—"

"I used to tell you a lot of things." She could still smell cigar smoke on his coat. "Leave me alone."

"I'll leave you alone," he said finally. "See how you like it."

She lay on the couch, her eyes fixed on a bowl of dead roses, until four o'clock in the afternoon. At four she called Les Goodwin.

"Something bad is going to happen to me," she said.

"Something bad is going to happen to all of us."

She could hear a typewriter in the background. "I mean it. Take me somewhere."

"You got a map of Peru?"

She said nothing.

"That's funny, Maria. That's a line from *Dark Passage*."

"I know it."

"I had a fight with Felicia at lunch, I've got to have a rewrite by tomorrow morning, I tell you something funny and you don't laugh."

"When I want to hear something funny I'll call you up again."

After she hung up she packed one bag and drove to he desert.

68

When I first married Carter and my name began appearing in columns I received mail from mad people. I am not much engaged by the problems of what you might call our day but I am burdened by the particular, the mad person who writes me a letter. It is no longer necessary for them even to write me. I know when someone is thinking of me. I learn to deal with this.

69

THE FIRST NIGHT in the still heat of the motel on the desert Carter turned away from Maria without speaking. The second night he got up and lay down on the bed in the other room.

"What's the matter," Maria said, standing in the doorway in the dark.

"It isn't any better."

"How do you know."

He said nothing.

"I mean we didn't even try."

"You don't want it."

"I do too."

"No," he said. "You don't."

Maria turned away. After that either she or Carter slept most nights in the other room. Some nights he said that he was tired, and some nights she said that she wanted to read, and other nights no one said anything.

In the motel on the desert there were the two

rooms, and a bathroom with a scaling metal shower stall, and a kitchenette with a few chipped dishes and an oilcloth-covered table. The air conditioner was broken, and through the open windows at night Maria could hear the jukebox from the bar across the road. On those nights when Carter could not sleep she lay perfectly still, her eyes closed, and waited for the moment when Carter would begin banging drawers, slamming doors, throwing a magazine across the bed where she lay.

"You aren't waking me up," she would say then. "I'm not asleep."

"Well *go* to sleep, cunt. Go to sleep. Die. Fucking vegetable."

After that point he would sleep. She would not.

By the time Maria woke at eight-thirty or nine in the morning it would already be 105°, 110°. Carter would be gone. For the first week Maria would wash in the trickle that came from the shower and drink a Coca-Cola in the bathroom and then drive out to the location, but on Monday of the second week Carter asked her to leave at lunchtime.

"You're making Susannah nervous," he said. "It's only her second picture, she's worried about working against Harrison, now you're here—the point is, when an actress is working, there's a certain—"

"I've worked once or twice. As an actress."

Carter avoided her eyes. "Maybe you and Helene could do something."

"Maybe we could see some plays."

70

THE TOWN WAS ON A DRY RIVER bed between Death
Valley and the Nevada line. Carter and BZ and Helene
and Susannah Wood and Harrison Porter and most of
the crew did not think of it as a town at all, but
Maria did: it was larger than Silver Wells. Besides
the motel, which was built of cinder block and oper-
ated by the wife of the sheriff's deputy who patrolled
the several hundred empty square miles around the
town, there were two gas stations, a store which sold
fresh meat and vegetables one day a week, a coffee
shop, a Pentecostal church, and the bar, which served
only beer. The bar was called The Rattler Room.
There was a bathhouse in the town, an aluminum
lean-to with a hot spring piped into a shallow concrete pool, and because of the hot baths the town
attracted old people, believers in cures and the restorative power of desolation, eighty- and ninety-
year-old couples who moved around the desert in
campers. There were a few dozen cinder-block houses

in the town, two trailer courts, and, on the dirt road that was the main street, the office for an abandoned talc mine called the Queen of Sheba. The office was boarded up. Fifty miles north there was supposed to be a school, but Maria saw no children.

"You can't call this a bad place," the woman who ran the coffee shop told Maria. The fan was broken and the door open and the woman swatted listlessly at flies. "I've lived in worse."

"So have I," Maria said. The woman shrugged.

By late day the thermometer outside the motel office would register between 120° and 130°. The old people put aluminum foil in their trailer windows to reflect the heat. There were two trees in the town, two cottonwoods in the dry river bed, but one of them was dead.

71

"You're with the movie," the boy at the gate to the bathhouse said. He was about eighteen and he had fair pimpled skin and he wore a straw field hat to ward off the sun. "I guessed it yesterday."

"My husband is."

"You want to know how I guessed?"

"How," Maria said.

"Because I—" The boy studied his grimy fingernails, as if no longer confident that the story illustrated a special acumen. "Because I personally know everybody from around here," he said then, his eyes on his fingernails. "I mean I guessed right away you weren't somebody I already knew."

"Actually I come from around here." Maria had spoken to no one else all day and she did not want to go into the bathhouse. She did not even know why she had come to the bathhouse. The bathhouse was full of old people, their loose skin pink from the water, sitting immobile on the edge of the pool nursing terminal cancers and wens and fear. "Actually I grew up in Silver Wells."

The boy looked at her impassively.

"It's across the line. I mean it's on the test range."

"How about that," the boy said, and then he leaned forward. "Your husband couldn't be Harrison Porter, could he?"

"No," Maria said, and then there seemed nothing more to say.

"My room, my game." Susannah Wood was sitting on her bed rolling cigarettes. "So turn up the sound."

Carter walked over to the bank of amplifiers and speakers and tape reels that Susannah had brought with her to the desert.

"Somebody's going to complain," Maria repeated.

"So what," Susannah Wood said, and then she laughed. "Maria thinks we're going to get arrested for possession. Maria thinks she's already *done* that number in Nevada."

BZ looked up. "Turn it down, Carter."

Susannah Wood looked first at BZ and then at Maria. "Turn it up, Carter."

Maria stood up. It was midnight and she was wearing only an old bikini bathing suit and her hair clung damply to the back of her neck. "I don't like any of you," she said. "You are all making me sick."

Susannah Wood laughed.

"That's not funny, Maria," Helene said.

"I mean sick. Physically sick."

Helene picked up a jar from the clutter on Susannah Wood's dressing table and began smoothing cream into Maria's shoulders. "If it's not funny don't say it, Maria."

"What about Susannah," Maria asked Carter. She was standing in the sun by the window brushing her hair.

"What about her."

Maria brushed her hair another twenty strokes and went into the bathroom. "I mean did you really like fucking her."

"Not particularly."

"I wonder why not," Maria said, and closed the bathroom door.

"Where's Carter," Maria said when she came into BZ's room.

"We had some trouble with Harrison, Carter stayed out there to block a scene with him. You want a drink?"

"I guess so. They coming back here?"

"I said we'd meet them in Vegas. Helene's there already."

"Let's not have dinner at the Riviera again."

"Harrison likes the Riviera."

Maria leaned back on Helene's bed. "I'm tired of Harrison." She licked the inside of her glass and let the bourbon coat her tongue. "Some ice might help."

"The refrigerator's broken. Roll a number."

Maria closed her eyes. "And I'm also tired of Susannah."

"What else are you tired of."

"I don't know."

"You're getting there," BZ said.

"Getting where."

"Where I am."

72

THEY HAD BEEN on the desert three weeks when Susannah Wood got beaten up in a hotel room in Las Vegas. The unit publicity man got over there right away and Harrison Porter did a surprise Telethon for Southern Nevada Cystic Fibrosis and there was no mention of the incident. When Maria asked Carter what had happened he shrugged.

"What difference does it make," he said.

Susannah Wood was not badly hurt but her face was bruised and she could not be photographed. Carter tried to shoot around her until the bruise was down enough to be masked by makeup but by the end of the fourth week they were running ten days over schedule.

"Was it Harrison?"

"It's over, she's O.K., drop it." Carter was standing by the window watching for BZ's car. BZ had been in town for meetings at the studio. "Susannah doesn't take things quite as hard as you do. So just forget it."

"Was it you?"

Carter looked at her. "You think that way, get your ass out of here."

In silence Maria pulled out a suitcase and began taking her clothes from hangers. In silence Carter watched her. By the time BZ walked in, neither of them had spoken for ten minutes.

"They're on your back," BZ said. He dropped his keys on the bed and took an ice tray from the refrigerator.

"I thought they liked the dailies."

"Ralph likes them. Kramer says they're very interesting."

"What does that mean."

"It means he wants to know why he's not seeing a master, two, closeup and reaction on every shot."

"If I started covering myself on every shot we'd bring it in at about two-five."

"All right, then, it doesn't mean that. It means he wants Ralph to hang himself with your rope." BZ looked at Maria. "What's she doing?"

"Ask her," Carter said, and walked out.

"Harrison did it," BZ said. "What's the problem."

"Carter was there. Wasn't Carter there."

"It was just something that got a little out of hand."

Maria sat down on the bed beside her suitcase. "Carter was there."

BZ looked at her for a long while and then laughed. "Of course Carter was there. He was there with Helene."

Maria said nothing.

"If you're pretending that it makes some difference to you, who anybody fucks and where and when and why, you're faking yourself."

"It does make a difference to me."

"No," BZ said. "It doesn't."

Maria stared out the window into the dry wash behind the motel.

"You know it doesn't. If you thought things like that mattered you'd be gone already. You're not going anywhere."

"Why don't you get me a drink," Maria said finally.

"What's the matter," Carter would ask when he saw her sitting in the dark at two or three in the morning staring out at the dry wash. "What do you want. I can't help you if you don't tell me what you want."

"I don't want anything."

"Tell me."

"I just told you."

"Fuck it then. Fuck it and fuck you. I'm up to here with you. I've had it. I've had it with the circles under your eyes and the veins showing on your arms and the lines starting on your face and your fucking menopausal depression—"

"Don't say that word to me."

"*Menopause. Old.* You're going to get *old.*"

"You talk crazy any more and I'll leave."

"Leave. For Christ's sake *leave.*"

She would not take her eyes from the dry wash. "All right."

"Don't," he would say then. "Don't."

"Why do you say those things. Why do you fight."

He would sit on the bed and put his head in his hands. "To find out if you're alive."

In the heat some mornings she would wake with her eyes swollen and heavy and she would wonder if she had been crying.

73

They had ten days left on the desert.

"Come out and watch me shoot today," Carter said.

"Later," she said. "Maybe later."

Instead she sat in the motel office and studied the deputy sheriff's framed photographs of highway accidents, imagined the moment of impact, tasted blood in her own dry mouth and searched the grain of the photographs with a magnifying glass for details not immediately apparent, the false teeth she knew must be on the pavement, the rattlesnake she suspected on the embankment. The next day she borrowed a gun from a stunt man and drove out to the highway and shot at road signs.

"That was edifying," Carter said. "Why'd you do it."

"I just did it."

"I want you to give that gun back to Farris."

"I already did."

"I don't want any guns around here."

Maria looked at him. "Neither do I," she said.

"I can't take any more of that glazed expression," Carter said. "I want you to wake up. I want you to come out with us today."

"Later," Maria said.

Instead she sat in the coffee shop and talked to the woman who ran it.

"I close down now until four," the woman said at two o'clock. "You'll notice it says that on the door, hours 6 a.m. to 2 p.m., 4 p.m. to—"

"6:30 p.m.," Maria said.

"Well. You saw it."

"What do you do between two and four."

"I go home, I usually—" The woman looked at Maria. "Look. You want to come out and see my place?"

The house was on the edge of the town, a trailer set on a concrete foundation. In place of a lawn there was a neat expanse of concrete, bordered by a split-rail fence, and beyond the fence lay a hundred miles of drifting sand.

"I got the only fence around here. Lee built it before he took off."

"Lee." Maria tried to remember in which of the woman's stories Lee had figured. "Where'd he go."

"Found himself a girl down to Barstow. I told you. Doreen Baker."

The sand was blowing through the rail fence onto

the concrete, drifting around the posts, coating a straight-backed chair with pale film. Maria began to cry.

"Honey," the woman said. "You pregnant or something?"

Maria shook her head and looked in her pocket for a Kleenex. The woman picked up a broom and began sweeping the sand into small piles, then edging the piles back to the fence. New sand blew in as she swept.

"You ever made a decision?" she said suddenly, letting the broom fall against the fence.

"About what."

"I made my decision in '61 at a meeting in Barstow and I never shed one tear since."

"No," Maria said. "I never did that."

74

When I was ten years old my father taught me to assess quite rapidly the shifting probabilities on a craps layout: I could trace a layout in my sleep, the field here and the pass line all around, even money on Big Six or Eight, five-for-one on Any Seven. Always when I play back my father's voice it is with a professional rasp, it goes as it lays, don't do it the hard way. My father advised me that life itself was a crap game: it was one of the two lessons I learned as a child. The other was that overturning a rock was apt to reveal a rattle-snake. As lessons go those two seem to hold up, but not to apply.

75

SHE SAT IN THE MOTEL in the late afternoon light looking out at the dry wash until its striations and shifting grains seemed to her a model of the earth and the moon. When BZ came in she did not look up.

"Let me entertain you," BZ said finally.

Maria said nothing.

"I could do my turn about Harrison calling one of the grips a vicious cunt."

"Please don't smoke in here, BZ."

"Why not."

She got up and filled a glass with the warm water from the tap. "Because it's a felony."

BZ laughed. Maria sat on the bed and drank the water and watched him roll a cigarette.

"I said don't, BZ."

"I get the feeling you want me to leave."

"I don't feel like talking to anybody."

"You don't have to talk to me." He lit the cigarette

and handed it to her. "You want to know where Carter is?"

"Still shooting."

"Maria, it's seven-thirty."

"I give up."

"He's with Helene."

"I thought I didn't have to talk to you."

"You aren't paying attention, Maria. Carter is fucking Helene. I thought these things made a big difference to you."

Maria got up and walked back to the window. In the few minutes that BZ had been distracting her the light had changed on the dry wash. Tomorrow she would borrow a camera, and station it on the dry wash for twenty-four hours.

"Tell me what matters," BZ said.

"Nothing," Maria said.

76

If Carter and Helene want to think it happened because I was insane, I say let them. They have to lay it off on someone. Carter and Helene still believe in cause-effect. Carter and Helene also believe that people are either sane or insane. Just once, the week after the desert, when Helene came to see me in Neuropsychiatric, I tried to explain how wrong she had been when she screamed that last night about my carelessness, my selfishness, my insanity, as if it had somehow slipped my attention what BZ was doing. I told her: there was no carelessness involved. Helene, I said: I knew precisely what BZ was doing. But Helene only screamed again.

Fuck it, I said to Helene. Fuck it, I said to them all, a radical surgeon of my own life. Never discuss. Cut. In that way I resemble the only man in Los Angeles County who does clean work.

77

"WHAT DO YOU THINK about it," Maria asked Carter.

"About what."

"What I just told you. About the man at the trailer camp who told his wife he was going out for a walk in order to talk to God."

"I wasn't listening, Maria. Just give me the punch line."

"There isn't any punch line, the highway patrol just found him dead, bitten by a rattlesnake."

"I'll say there isn't any punch line."

"Do you think he talked to God?"

Carter looked at her.

"I mean do you think God answered? Or don't you?"

Carter walked out of the room.

The heat stuck. The air shimmered. An underground nuclear device was detonated where Silver Wells had once been, and Maria got up before dawn to feel the blast. She felt nothing.

"I'm giving this one more chance," Carter said when

he saw her sitting by the window. "Tell me what you want."

"Nothing."

"I want to help you. Tell me what you feel."

She looked at the hand he held out to her. "Nothing," she said.

"You say that again and I swear to Christ—"

She shrugged. He left the motel.

They had three days left on the desert.

78

*Except when they let Carter or Helene in, I never
minded Neuropsychiatric and I don't mind here.
Nobody bothers me. The only problem is Kate. I
want Kate.*

79

"WE SHOT THE LAST MASTER after you left this afternoon," Carter said when he came in with Helene. "Three set-ups in the morning and we're home. Fantastic."

"Susannah was fabulous," Helene said. "Supergood."

BZ said nothing. Maria stared out the window.

"You should have seen Carter working with her."

"I bet he was fabulous," BZ said. "Fab."

80

The one time Ivan Costello got through the switch-board to me here he told me that I had lost my sense of humor. In spite of what Carter and Helene think, maybe my sense of humor was all I did lose.

81

"YOU WERE FANTASTIC TODAY," Helene said when Susannah Wood came in.

"Super-good," BZ said. "Really key."

Susannah Wood lay down on Maria's bed. "Let's go into Vegas."

"It's all planned." Helene did not look at BZ. "Sylvie Roth's over, and Cassie and Leona and—"

BZ stood up. "You go into Vegas."

"Don't you want to see Sylvie?"

"No."

"Don't you want to see Leona's last show?"

"No."

The cords tightened on Helene's neck. "Exactly what do you want."

Susannah Wood giggled. "I saw the charts today, Leona's single stopped at 85."

BZ looked at Helene. "Exactly nothing," he said pleasantly.

Maria dropped a tray of ice on the floor.

82

Carter and Helene still ask questions. I used to ask questions, and I got the answer: nothing. The answer is "nothing." Now that I have the answer, my plans for the future are these: (1) get Kate, (2) live with Kate alone, (3) do some canning. Damson plums, apricot preserves. Sweet India relish and pickled peaches. Apple chutney. Summer squash succotash. There might even be a ready market for such canning: you will note that after everything I remain Harry and Francine Wyeth's daughter and Benny Austin's godchild. For all I know they knew the answer too, and pretended they didn't. You call it as you see it, and stay in the action. BZ thought otherwise. If Carter and Helene aren't careful they'll get the answer too.

83

"I THOUGHT YOU'D BE in Vegas," BZ said when Maria opened the door. He was holding a bottle of vodka and in spite of the heat he was wearing a blazer and a tie. "With Carter and Helene and Susannah and Harrison and Sylvia and Cassie and Leona and—"

"You knew I wasn't going." Maria lay down on the bed again.

"All right, I knew." He sat on the edge of the bed and loosened his tie. "Look at me all duded up. Why are you in bed at nine o'clock."

"Why not."

"Beautiful."

Maria looked at him. "Tell me why you're sad."

"You're a good girl." All the musculature seemed gone from BZ's face. He put down the bottle of vodka and reached into his pocket. "You know what these are?"

He poured twenty or thirty capsules onto the bed before she answered.

"Grain-and-a-half Seconal."

"You want some?"

She looked at him. "No."

"You're still playing." BZ did not take his eyes from hers. "Some day you'll wake up and you just won't feel like playing any more."

"That's a queen's way of doing it."

"I never expected you to fall back on style as an argument."

"I'm not arguing."

"I know that. You think I'd be here if I didn't know that?"

She took his hand and held it. "Why are you here."

"Because you and I, we *know* something. Because we've been out there where nothing is. Because I wanted—you know why."

"Lie down here," she said after a while. "Just go to sleep."

When he lay down beside her the Seconal capsules rolled on the sheet. In the bar across the road somebody punched *King of the Road* on the jukebox again, and there was an argument outside, and the sound of a bottle breaking. Maria held onto BZ's hand.

"Listen to that," he said. "Try to think about having enough left to break a bottle over it."

"It would be very pretty," Maria said. "Go to sleep."

211

She was almost asleep when she sensed that his weight had shifted.

"*Don't.*" After she had said it she opened her eyes.

He was swallowing the capsules with a glass of water. There were not very many left on the bed.

"Don't start faking me now." BZ turned off the light and lay down again. "Take my hand. Go back to sleep."

"I'm sorry," she said after a while.

"Hold onto me," BZ said.

When Maria woke again the room was blazing with light and Carter was shaking her and Helene was screaming. Maria thought she had never heard anyone scream the way Helene screamed. She closed her eyes against the light and her ears against Helene and her mind against what was going to happen in the next few hours and tightened her hold on BZ's hand.

84

Carter called today, but I saw no point in talking to him. On the whole I talk to no one. I concentrate on the way light would strike filled Mason jars on a kitchen windowsill. I lie here in the sunlight, watch the hummingbird. This morning I threw the coins in the swimming pool, and they gleamed and turned in the water in such a way that I was almost moved to read them. I refrained.

One thing in my defense, not that it matters: I know something Carter never knew, or Helene, or maybe you. I know what "nothing" means, and keep on playing.

Why, BZ would say.

Why not, I say.

ABOUT THE AUTHOR